THE KIMBERLEY SECRET

A Historical Mystery Novella

"Before it all began …"

GABRIEL FARAGO

This book is brought to you by Bear & King Publishing.

Publishing & Marketing Consultant: Lama Jabr
Website: https://xanapublishingandmarketing.com/
Sydney, Australia

Cover Design by Giovanni Banfi

First published 2018 © Gabriel Farago

CONTENTS

AUTHOR'S NOTE

In December 2017, everything changed for me as an author. *The Hidden Genes of Professor K* – Book 3 in the *Jack Rogan Mysteries Series* – had just been voted 'Outstanding Thriller of the Year' by the Independent Author Network (IAN) in the US. This gave the book huge publicity and exposure worldwide, and created a lot of interest in Jack Rogan – the central character – and the series generally.

Then just before Christmas, I received a phone call from my publicist, Lama. 'We're getting a lot of enquiries about Jack,' she said.

We had both received many emails from readers wanting to know more about Jack's earlier life; what had shaped his character, and how he became the 'incorrigible rascal' my readers appear to love so much.

'Good to hear,' I said. 'It shows we are engaging with them and creating interest in the series.'

'True, but they all want to know more about Jack.'

I suspected at once where this was heading. 'What's on your mind?' I asked with some trepidation.

'Remember last time we rewarded your readers and subscribers with a free novella?' Lama said.

'Of course, *The Forgotten Painting*,' I replied. 'It was very well received.'

'Exactly. We should do it again.'

'What do you mean?'

'Reward your readers for their loyalty and support, and at the same time pique their interest in the next book we are about to release by giving them what they are asking for.'

'And what might that be?'

'Another novella telling your readers more about Jack, his childhood, his family; in short, what makes him tick. And we should link it all to the books in the series generally.'

'Is *that* all? Are you serious? You want me to write a novella? *Now?*

I'm still finalising the next book, and about to go away for Christmas,' I protested. 'I promised my wife—'

'Come on, you will enjoy it!' Lama coaxed, casually brushing my concerns aside. 'And one more thing,' she added. 'Make it a page-turner.'

And then she did something she has done many times before. She hung up on me.

I spent Christmas in New Zealand and thought a lot about all this during long walks through primeval rainforests and along the shores of pristine mountain lakes. All of my ideas for books seem to start that way.

I had done some research last year in the remote Kimberley wilderness in Western Australia with a novella about Jack Rogan's earlier life in mind, but that was for *later*, not right now. However, in publishing, timing is everything, and deep down I knew Lama was right. Releasing a novella before the next book was published was definitely the right way to go, and Lama realised of course that I would come 'round. Eventually.

So, that's how it all began. I must admit that once I started writing, everything fell into place and I enjoyed delving into Jack's earlier life and secrets immensely! But please don't tell Lama this!

However, before you start reading, just a few words about the novella as a literary genre:

The novella made its first appearance in the early Renaissance, especially in Italy and in France. Giovanny Boccaccio's *The Decameron* (1335), and *Heptameron* (1559), penned by the French queen Marguerite de Navarre and modelled on *The Decameron*, were the trailblazers. However, it wasn't until the late 18th and early 19th centuries that the novella took shape as the literary genre we know today.

Robert Silverberg in Sailing to Byzantium *describes the novella as:* "one of the richest and most rewarding of literary forms ... it allows for more extended development of theme and character than does the short story, without making the elaborate structural demands of the full-length book. Thus it provides an intense, detailed exploration of its subject, providing to some degree both the concentrated focus of the short story and the broad scope of the novel."

Silverberg, Robert (2000). *Sailing to Byzantium.* New York; ibooks, inc. ISBN 0-7861-99059

The Kimberley Secret is a novella, and as such, it is of course much shorter than my novels, but without losing focus or scope. That was one of the reasons I have chosen this genre as the vehicle to explore certain aspects of Jack Rogan's earlier life, and reveal a little more about his background and character.

Gabriel Farago
Leura, Blue Mountains, May 2018

Battle of Takur Ghar: 4 March 2002

Operation Anaconda was in full swing. Australian and coalition forces were locked in a fierce battle with the Taliban and al-Qaeda in the Paktia Province in Afghanistan. Pressing his precious camera to his flak jacket, Jack Rogan hit the ground as heavy machine-gun fire erupted from one of the caves on his right. This was soon followed by mortar fire from above. The battle raged for hours in the difficult terrain, riddled with heavily fortified caves and bunkers, but by nightfall, the Shai-Kot Valley had been secured. According to US estimates, between 500 and 800 rebel fighters had been killed.

Working as an experienced freelance war correspondent with an impressive track record – especially in sensitive hotspots in Africa – Jack had quickly earned the respect of the US forces operating in Afghanistan. Fearless, and maintaining his sense of humour even in the most dangerous situations, Jack's easy-going – at times almost laconic – manner had endeared him to many of the fighters at the front. His photographs were legendary and his articles sought after by leading newspapers and magazines all over the world. His Voices from the Front Line articles were balanced and incisive, without sensationalising or over-dramatising events. Jack told it how he saw it, and he made sure he was right there where it all happened. His reporting had a raw, often quite confronting eyewitness quality that showed war as it really was: brutal, unforgiving, and often totally senseless and inhuman.

As soon as the guns fell silent, Jack took off his helmet, pulled his notebook out of his backpack and sat down on a rock ledge overlooking the valley. With the pungent smell of cordite and death still hanging in the air, he began to jot down his impressions of the battle he had just witnessed. Jack knew that to capture the authenticity of the moment was the most important part of his work; it gave his articles the edge. The next most important thing was timing. Still high on adrenaline, there was an almost feverish energy pulsating through Jack as he described the dramatic events of the past few hours. He knew that the newspaper which had commissioned the articles was standing by, waiting for his call. But before he could contact his editor in the US, his satellite phone rang inside his backpack.

The reception wasn't good. Distorted by interference and constant crackling, the voice on the other end of the line sounded distant and could barely be heard.

'Yes, yes. This is Jack Rogan,' Jack almost shouted. 'Who are you? Where are you calling from?'

'The Felicitas Boarding House in Townsville. It's about your father,' said the voice.

'What did you say?'

'Your father.'

'What about him?'

'He wants to see you.'

'I'm in Afghanistan, in the middle of a war,' Jack said impatiently.

'He's dying.'

By calling in favours, Jack managed to hitch a ride on a helicopter taking the wounded back to Kabul. Leaving the barracks, he went straight to the room he rented near Bala Hissar, an ancient fortress to the south of the modern city centre, and quickly packed his duffel bag. Then he called a contact at the airport and made travel arrangements to take him home to Australia.

Waiting for his connecting flight in Singapore, Jack took a long shower at the airport and tried to get some sleep in the lounge. He had been travelling for many hours and felt drained and exhausted. However, the much-needed sleep wouldn't come. Instead, memories of his childhood kept him awake as his mind drifted back to turbulent times spent on a remote cattle station in outback Queensland, where life was as harsh as the relentless sun and as unforgiving as the drought that punished the land all too often, causing unimaginable hardship and despair.

For a son to travel home after a long absence to see his dying father for the last time was a tough call, even for a battle-hardened war correspondent like Jack. Memories reach secret corners of the heart and stir up long-forgotten emotions that can easily overwhelm the unwary.

By the time Jack stepped off the plane in Townsville and caught a taxi to the modest boarding house on the outskirts of town, he thought he had steeled himself for the painful encounter he knew he was about to face. He had seen death in many guises, often too violent and brutal to photograph or describe. Death was never pretty. But when Jack entered his father's darkened room and looked at the emaciated, motionless shell of a man staring into space, his heart sank and tears began to well up, impossible to suppress.

For a while Jack stood quietly by the door, trying to compose himself as he stared at that mountain of a man he used to admire, now reduced by deadly cancer to a crumbling hill about to turn to dust.

'Dad?' whispered Jack, choking with emotion.

His father turned his head towards his son as his eyes began to focus. 'Jack?'

'It's me,' said Jack. He walked over to the bed, sat down on the edge and reached for his father's limp hand.

'Good to see you, mate. Back from the war?' said his father, his voice growing stronger.

Jack nodded.

'I've got to tell you something important. There isn't much time ...'

'What?'

'This will come as a bit of a shock, but you have to know,' said his father, squeezing Jack's hand. 'I've had a lot of time to think about this, lying here. How to tell you ...'

'What are you talking about?'

'I've always loved you as my own ...'

Jack looked at his father and wondered where this was going.

'But you're not,' continued his father, his voice growing faint.

'I don't understand.'

His father took a deep breath – his chest heaving – and looked at Jack. 'You're not my son; you're not *our* son.'

Jack looked confused. *He's delirious*, he thought, certain he had misunderstood.

'You were brought to us as a baby. You were so tiny; only a few days old. Mum couldn't have children. It was the tragedy of her life. It's what drove her away. That and other things ...'

'Jesus, Dad! What are you saying?' demanded Jack as the words began to sink in.

'We took you into our hearts and our home. We thought you were a precious gift – the answer to our prayers.'

He's serious, thought Jack, his mind racing. *Could this be true?* 'You're not kidding, are you?' he said.

'No. I agonised over this for a long time. Whether to tell you ...'

'So, why did you? What difference does it make today? You and Mum are my parents. Always have been. Always will be,' said Jack, tears in his eyes.

'It's not that simple.

'Isn't it?'

'I believe you are entitled to know who you are.'

'I know who I am.'

'Perhaps. But the truth is still the truth, whichever way we look at it.'

'And you are just going to leave this here? Just like that? Or are you going to tell me more?'

'There isn't much more I can tell you. We never found out who your biological parents were.'

'What, I just appeared at your doorstep out of nowhere? Is that it?'

'Just about.'

'Come on, Dad ... *How?*

'Someone brought you to our home ...'

'Who?' demanded Jack.

'Gurrul.'

Gurrul was an Aboriginal stockman who had worked at the Rogan family cattle station all his life. He had been Jack's friend and mentor ever since Jack could remember.

'So, he would know?'

'Where you came from? Who your parents ...?' Obviously exhausted, Jack's father closed his eyes and his voice became weaker. 'Yes, I believe he would know,' he whispered. 'But he made a promise ...'

'What promise?'

'He promised not to tell, and we had to promise not to ask.'

'Did you?'

'Yes.'

Jack realised time was running out fast. 'Is there anything else you can tell me? About where I came from, I mean.'

'This may help,' said his father and pointed to a piece of paper on the bedside table. 'Give it to me.'

Jack picked up the paper and gave it to his father. 'What's this?' he asked.

'When you came to us, wrapped in a towel, you had something around your neck. Something beautiful and precious.'

'What?'

'When things got really tough during one of the terrible droughts, I took it to—'

'What was it, Dad? *Tell me*!' interrupted Jack. 'You took it where?'

His father opened his eyes and looked at Jack for the last time. It was a look Jack would never forget; a look of bittersweet love and regret. Then his father's eyes began to glaze over as his mind drifted back to his beloved homestead he had inherited from his father. 'I have only one regret,' he whispered. 'I lost our land, the cattle, our home, your inheritance ... the link to our past ...'

For a terrible moment, Jack's father's breathing became violent. He was gasping for breath like a man drowning and stared at Jack with unseeing eyes as the grip of death tightened around his emaciated chest, squeezing life out of his disease-riddled body. Then suddenly, it was over and everything stopped.

For a while, Jack just sat there in silence, tears streaming down his ashen face. Then he reached across, closed his father's eyes and began to pray. It was a little prayer his mother had taught him as a boy. Not a religious man, Jack hadn't prayed in years, but somehow the simple, familiar words seemed to comfort him. When he leaned across to kiss his father's forehead, he noticed the piece of paper he had handed to him earlier. Jack took the paper gently out of his father's hand and looked at it. It was a receipt issued by a pawnbroker in Brisbane.

THE FUNERAL: 11 MARCH 2002

Despite pressing deadlines and numerous phone calls from his impatient editors in Sydney and the US, Jack stayed in Townsville to make funeral arrangements and finalise his father's affairs.

Old men's funerals are often lonely occasions. Jack realised that most of his father's mates had either passed away, or were in nursing homes, too ill to travel. As Jack had no siblings and the extended Irish family was very small and certainly not close, there was no-one Jack had to notify. However, he did place a death notice in the paper, just in case. His estranged mother had left the remote homestead and her marriage a long time ago, and had passed away in Cairns after a short illness while Jack was still a young cadet, struggling to become a journalist.

Jack's closest friend – Will Elliott – who would certainly have come to the funeral, was in hospital recovering from injuries he had sustained in a recent bushfire. Jack had lived with the Elliott family in Sydney during his cadet years and had shared many an adventure with Will and his dad during that time.

Because his father had been a religious man, Jack arranged a small service in a Catholic church near the crematorium.

Jack had bought a dark suit and black tie on the weekend, and was steeling himself for what he knew would be a difficult and emotional occasion, made doubly heart-wrenching because there would be no-one there to share it with him. The priest understood and had been very helpful. He promised to keep the service short.

The funeral was due to start at eleven. Ignoring the light rain and oppressive humidity, Jack stood in front of the church to wait for the hearse. He was determined to be one of the pallbearers to carry his father's coffin into the church. Apart from two old men seated inside, who had arrived from a nursing home earlier with their walking frames and a carer, the church was empty.

I don't know if I can do this, thought Jack, overwhelmed by the sadness of the moment as the hearse pulled up and the undertakers began to lift the modest coffin out of the back. Biting his lip and forcing back tears, Jack walked slowly over to the hearse.

As he was about to take his place next to the undertakers carrying the coffin, Jack heard a voice call out from behind: 'We'll do this together, mate.'

Jack spun around. '*You? Here?*' he said, astonished. 'How?' He hadn't seen Gurrul since Jack had left the family cattle station as a teenager.

The elderly Aboriginal nodded. 'Saw the notice on the weekend. Just made it. Let's take him inside.'

With that, Gurrul shouldered the coffin alongside Jack at the front. Jack glanced at the familiar face next to him. Furrowed like the parched outback earth, and with deep creases and wrinkles crisscrossing his forehead that looked as if they could hold three days' rain, the face had changed a little, but the eyes were the same, radiating intelligence and kindness.

'Thanks, mate,' whispered Jack as they entered the church. 'You were always there when I needed you most,' he added, no longer feeling quite so sad and alone.

'You reckon we can call this a wake?' said Jack, raising his glass. 'Just the two of us?'

'Sure, mate,' replied Gurrul. 'We've just been to a funeral to send-off someone we both loved, and we're in a pub having a beer. It's a wake all right. Cheers.'

Over the next hour, Jack and Gurrul chatted about the past, and the direction their lives had taken since Jack had left home and gone to work for a paper in Brisbane.

'You've done all right, mate,' said Gurrul. 'I've read some of your articles over the years. Love your *Voices from the Front Line*. Not bad for a kid from the bush.'

'What about you?'

Gurrul put down his glass and looked at Jack. 'A couple of years after you left, things got really bad.'

'The drought?'

Gurrul nodded. 'Tough times.'

'Mum left and the bank took the farm,' said Jack. 'I know ...'

'It broke your old man.'

'I was living in Sydney by then, working for the *Herald*.' Jack pointed to Gurrul's empty glass. 'Another?' he asked, trying to change the painful subject.

'He understood.'

'Why I had to leave?'

'Yes. And that made it even harder ...'

Jack ordered two more beers. 'What about you? Where did you go?' he asked.

'Here and there. I went back to the mission and worked there until it was closed down. After that, I became a drifter. There was always work for someone like me.' Gurrul looked pensively into his glass. 'But it was never the same again ...'

Gurrul had grown up on the Coberg Mission, not far from the Rogan cattle station. He received all his schooling there while his parents and older siblings went walkabout. The nuns gave him a good, basic education and the brothers taught him how to work with his hands. That's where he had met Jack's father, who offered him a job when Gurrul turned fifteen.

'And now? What are you doing now?' asked Jack.

'Look at me. I've become an old man. I went back to my roots.'

'Roots? Where?'

'The Kimberley; my country. Our mob came from up there.'

'I didn't know. You never spoke about it.'

'I wanted to belong elsewhere. Your dad's cattle station was my home for years.'

'I understand. So, we both buried the past today, you think?'

'We did. Do you want to know what I'm doing in the Kimberley?'

'Sure.'

'Don't laugh.'

'I won't.'

'I'm restoring paintings – ancient rock art. In the bush.'

'Are you serious?'

'Absolutely, mate. It's tradition. My tribe has done this forever. The Kimberley is full of stunning rock paintings, many of them thousands of years old. Some of them fifty thousand. Even more, some experts reckon.'

Jack looked at Gurrul, surprised.

'We old folk are the custodians responsible for preserving the paintings for future generations and keeping them in good order. We are also telling the Dreamtime stories to the young ones, around the campfire. I've become a storyteller just like you, mate. That's what I do now, as an elder. I move around a lot, of course. Going from one sacred site to the next, but I have a place in Wyndham. One of my nephews lives there. That's where I saw the death notice. I hitched a ride in one of the cattlemen's planes, and here I am.'

'But that's fabulous,' said Jack, his curiosity aroused. 'Bradshaw paintings, Wandjina art?'

It was Gurrul's turn to look surprised. 'You know about stuff like this?'

'A little.'

'Not bad for a war correspondent.'

Jack looked at the empty beer glasses on the table. It was time to ask the question that had been haunting him throughout the funeral.

'Do you believe in destiny?' said Jack.

'Why do you ask?'

'Because I believe destiny has brought us together. Today, at the funeral.'

'How come?'

Jack reached into his pocket and pulled out the pawnbroker's receipt his father had held in his hand when he died. 'Because of this,' he said and handed the receipt to Gurrul.

Gurrul looked at the receipt. 'I don't follow,' he said.

'You will in a moment. In fact, I believe you hold the key to all this.'

'Please explain.'

'Just before he died, Dad told me something that rocked me, but will come as no surprise to you ...'

'Oh?'

'Mum couldn't have children. It was the tragedy of her life. So, you brought her one: *me.*'

For a while the two men sat in silence, engrossed in memories.

'He told you,' said Gurrul.

'He did.'

'What else did he tell you? About where you came from.'

'Not much. He said you promised not to tell, and he promised not to ask.'

Gurrul nodded. 'Some things are best left alone, mate.'

Jack shook his head. 'I can't do that; not now.'

'Suppose not.'

'So, what else can you tell me? You didn't just find me under a rock in the outback?'

'Of course not. I shouldn't have come ...'

'Yet here you are.'

'You were born at the Coberg Mission,' said Gurrul after a while, looking troubled.

'You're kidding. The place was full of old Pallottine brothers and nuns.'

'True, but there was a young woman staying with them at the time. A pretty lass in her early twenties. Remember Brother Francis?'

'Of course; how could I forget?'

'Well, he and Sister Elizabeth seemed to know her well. She was pregnant when she arrived and stayed at the mission until her baby was born. She left after that.'

'And she left the baby behind?'

Gurrul nodded.

'And you gave it to—'

'I did. With the blessing of Brother Francis and Sister Elizabeth. They knew your mum and dad would give the child love and a good home. They were right.'

'That's it?'

Gurrul shrugged.

'Who was the young woman?'

'Don't know.'

'What about the father?'

Gurrul pulled his tobacco pouch out of his pocket and began to roll a cigarette with yellow-stained fingers. 'A couple of years after you were born, Brother Francis told me something ...'

'What?'

'He said something terrible had happened concerning the father of the baby; your father.'

'Did he say what it was?'

'I remember he was very upset. He had the paper right in front of him and was pointing to the headlines.'

'What was it about?'

'A court case. A sensational murder trial – in Perth.'

'You're kidding.'

'I wish I was.'

'And it concerned the baby's – *my* – father?'

'Apparently so.'

'Do you remember a name?'

Inhaling deeply, Gurrul shrugged. 'Not a name, but I remember the case was all about a famous pearl.'

'A pearl?'

'Yes.'

'Do you remember what paper he was reading?'

'*The Courier Mail* from Brisbane; what else?'

'My old paper. Can you be more specific about the year?'

'I reckon it was around 1970. Yes, I think it was 1970. We just had a big bushfire. That's why I was at the mission; helping to fight it. Yes, January, or early February 1970.'

'Incredible. What about the young woman? *My mother*?'

'Can't tell you much, I'm afraid. All I know is she left as soon as the baby was born and returned to Europe.'

Jack pointed to the pawnbroker receipt on the bar in front of him. 'Dad told me I had something around my neck when I arrived. Something beautiful and precious he called it. Can you remember what it was?'

'Yes. A little gold cross with precious stones. Apparently, it belonged to your mother.'

'Which Dad took to the pawnshop in 1972 when times got tough?'

'I don't know anything about that.'

Jack stabbed his finger at the receipt. 'Here, look at this. Two thousand bucks for a piece of jewellery? Quite a tidy sum at the time, wouldn't you say? You could have bought a Holden station wagon with that.'

'True.'

'Dad was trying to tell me something just before he died. Something important about this.'

'Looks that way.'

Jack ordered another round of beers. 'A sensational court case in Perth in 1970, and a precious little gold cross left in a pawnshop in Brisbane in 1972 is all we have to go by?' he mused.

'That's about it. I'd leave it alone if I were you, mate,' said Gurrul, putting an arm around Jack. 'Not much, is it?'

'Perhaps not, but it's a start.'

THE PAWNBROKER: 12 MARCH 2002

Jack felt strangely relieved after the funeral. It was as if a dark cloud had been lifted from his soul. The day he had dreaded for so long was over. He had buried his father and closed a painful chapter in his life. However, finding out that he had been adopted shortly after birth under rather mysterious circumstances, had been quite a shock. Jack believed that fate had thrown some important clues his way, pointing him in a certain direction. It was now up to him to follow the breadcrumbs of destiny to find out the truth about who he really was, and where he had come from.

Gurrul had flown back to Wyndham early the next morning, and Jack caught a plane to Brisbane to follow his first lead: the pawnbroker.

Jack showed the taxi driver the address on the receipt.

'Is this it?' he asked as the taxi pulled up in front of a small sandwich bar in a working-class suburb on the outskirts of Brisbane.

'That's it. Number twelve; right there.'

Jack paid the fare, got out of the taxi and walked inside the shop, unable to suppress a feeling of disappointment. *Hardly surprising after all these years*, he thought. *Looks like a dead end. Bugger!*

The man behind the counter remembered the pawnshop, which had closed its doors many years ago. But when Jack turned to leave, the man told him that the old pawnbroker still owned the premises and lived in the cottage next door.

'If he doesn't answer the doorbell, he's probably in the backyard with his birds,' said the man. 'There's a side gate. You'll have to speak loudly as he's almost deaf. His name is Ross McGregor; funny chap.'

Jack thanked the man, went next door and pressed the doorbell. There was no answer. Then he walked around the house, unlatched the side gate and followed the gravel path into the backyard. As he rounded the corner, Jack stopped. The large backyard was like a tropical paradise. Shaded by tall palm trees and Queensland pittosporum, the mature, carefully laid out garden was a riot of colour. Beds of yellow, white and pink hibiscus and other colourful natives framed the walkway leading past a pond into what looked like a small rainforest. Along the fence at the back, Jack could make out a tall aviary surrounded by tree ferns. Inside the shaded, mysterious aviary, exotic birds were screeching for attention. A man sat in a wicker chair in front of the aviary, his face covered by a straw hat. He appeared to be asleep.

'Mr McGregor?' said Jack.

The man in the chair didn't move.

'Mr McGregor,' repeated Jack, raising his voice.

The man in the chair began to stir. He pushed back his hat and looked at Jack. 'Who are you?' he said gruffly.

Jack reached into his pocket and took out the receipt. 'Jack Rogan. I've come about this,' he said, handing the receipt to the man.

Shielding his eyes from the glare of the sun, the man peered at the receipt. 'You took your time,' he said. 'What do you want?'

'It's a long story.'

'Pull up a chair and tell me.'

McGregor listened attentively as Jack told him what he knew about the little gold cross with the precious stones. He began with his father's funeral the day before, how he had obtained the receipt, and why he was following up the matter.

At first McGregor didn't say anything after Jack had finished. Then he handed the receipt back to him. 'That's quite a story, young man,' he said. 'I suppose you would like to know what happened to the cross?'

Jack nodded.

'As a matter of fact, I do remember it well. It was a rare piece; very special. A collector's item.'

'In what way?'

'If you come into the aviary and help me feed the birds, I'll tell you.'

'You're on.'

McGregor handed Jack a large steel tray divided into various compartments filled with all kinds of seeds and nuts, and opened a narrow screen door.

'Come; hurry!' he said.

Jack followed him into the aviary and McGregor quickly shut the screen door behind him as the screeching inside became louder and more urgent.

'These are my special friends. Magnificent, aren't they?'

'Absolutely,' said Jack, as a flash of bright colour landed on the edge of his tray, followed by another landing on his shoulder.

'Cheeky lorikeets; always have to be first. Don't worry about them.'

McGregor pointed to a low branch above a small pond. 'There, look at him. A palm cockatoo from Cape York; very rare.'

Jack looked at the large bird with its enormous bill, striking red face and the many-feathered upright crest. It looked like a print out of a John Gould portfolio.

'Amazing!'

'He's almost as rare as that little cross you are so interested in.'

'Why was it so rare?'

'Well, it wasn't often that a genuine Fabergé piece came into my shop. But that was exactly what it was. An original Fabergé, handcrafted by Alexander Fabergé in Paris in 1933. Among other things, it had a date stamp. But there was more ...'

'What do you mean?'

'It had a unique design. This was no ordinary cross. This was a cus-tom-made, Russian Orthodox cross with three horizontal crossbeams,' said McGregor, warming to his subject. 'The bottom one, the footrest, was slanted upwards.'

'Do you know why?'

'Yes, because the side to Christ's right is often depicted higher as it points to the penitent thief Saint Dismas, who was crucified on Jesus' right. But the other thief, Gestas on Jesus' left, was impenitent. That's why the footrest points downward, to Hades. Obviously, the Fabergé client wanted to have this incorporated into the design.'

'Fascinating.'

McGregor extended his arm and whistled. A large red, black-billed parrot, with a blue belly and shoulders, landed on his hand almost im-mediately. 'An eclectus parrot, also from Cape York,' said McGregor. 'This is the female. Aren't you beautiful, my love,' cooed McGregor.

'The House of Fabergé was founded in St Petersburg in 1842,' he continued, stroking the wing of the bird with his other hand. 'It was best-known for designing the famous jewel-encrusted Fabergé eggs for the Russian Tsars until it was nationalised by the Bolsheviks in 1918. The little cross was of the same quality and workmanship. In the nineteen twenties, Alexander Fabergé and his half-brother Eugene opened *Fabergé et Cie* in Paris. The little cross dated from that period.'

'Wow,' said Jack, impressed. 'You certainly know your Fabergé.'

'I'm a jeweller by trade and have an eye for such things,' explained McGregor. 'Trained in Glasgow with someone who knew a lot about Fabergé. It was very valuable; exquisite stones.'

'Do you know what happened to it?' asked Jack, taking a deep breath.

'It was sold, of course.'

'To whom?'

McGregor looked at Jack and shook his head. 'It was a long time ago. My shop's been closed for ten years or more.' McGregor saw the disappointment on Jack's face and smiled. 'The birds like you,' he said. 'Look!' Two more birds – a pair of noisy cockatiels – landed on Jack's shoulders and began to nibble his ear.

'They don't take to everyone, you know.'

Jack nodded, carefully balancing the tray in his hands. He suspected that his popularity had more to do with the tray of food than the magnetism of his personality.

'Cheer up. I will try to dig out my records. I still have them. They are in the shed over there. The receipt has a number and a date. That should help.'

Feeling relieved, Jack watched McGregor fill up the little food trays scattered around the aviary. During the next fifteen minutes, Jack was introduced to a stunning blue-winged kookaburra, several Australian king parrots, a huge red-tailed black cockatoo from Arnhem Land called Harry, and a sacred kingfisher from Victoria. After that, McGregor made some tea and then retired to his shed to find the records.

Jack looked at his watch. McGregor had been most helpful. It was just after noon. It had taken Jack less than an hour to identify the man who purchased the Fabergé gold cross from McGregor in October 1976.

Bernard Lloyd. How amazing, thought Jack, shaking his head.

Bernard Lloyd AO, was a famous painter and one of Australia's most acclaimed living artists. His paintings were displayed in major galleries around the world and graced the boardrooms of banks and mining giants. One of his best-known works hung in the foyer of Parliament House in Canberra. Lloyd was an eccentric recluse who lived on a small farm in the Southern Highlands not far from Sydney. Jack realised that getting to meet him wouldn't be easy. That was for another day. As he had five hours to spare before his flight home to Sydney, Jack decided to pay his old paper, the *Courier Mail,* a quick visit. Founded in 1846, the *Courier Mail* was one of Australia's oldest newspapers. Jack had got his first job there after he left home at seventeen. What began with sweeping floors and running errands, had turned into a cadetship and ultimately, a successful international career.

Jack smiled as the taxi stopped in front of the familiar building on the corner of Mayne Road and Campbell Street, Bowen Hills, a Brisbane suburb.

Jack had kept in touch with several journalists and editors over the years, and many of Jack's articles and photographs had featured in the paper. His *Voices from the Front Line* articles were particularly popular. He therefore had no difficulty in gaining access to the paper's extensive archives and enlisted the help of a senior archivist, a lady in her late sixties called Maud Featherstone. Maud, a feisty spinster, had worked at the paper for almost fifty years and knew Jack well.

Maud's eyes lit up as Jack walked up to her desk in the basement. Jack gave her a big hug and explained what he was after.

'So, you want to know about a court case in Perth in early 1970?' she said, taking notes. 'Research?'

'Something like that. Apparently there was a front-page article about the case, possibly more, in January or early February that year; a sensational murder trial involving a pearl ... I don't have any names.'

'*A pearl?* How curious. Shouldn't be too difficult to find. Why don't you go to the cafeteria for a chinwag with the boys while I ferret around a little?'

'Just like the old days – eh?'

'Some things never change.'

'Your blood's worth bottling,' said Jack, giving Maud a peck on the cheek.

Maud came looking for Jack in the cafeteria half an hour later.

'Any luck?' asked Jack.

'It was all over the papers for a couple of weeks. Front-page news. Quite a case.' Maud handed Jack an envelope. 'Here, I've copied the articles for you.'

'Who was the accused?' asked Jack, holding his breath.

'A young man called Bryn Evans, a pearl diver from Broome.'

The Painter in the Bush: 14 March 2002

Frustrated, Jack pulled over and looked again at the creased map on his lap. The GPS had stopped being helpful as soon as he drove through the last village on the map, and he was now feeling his way along a narrow dirt road leading into the bush.

This guy must really like his privacy, thought Jack, shaking his head. *This is the middle of nowhere.* The directions he had been given by Lloyd's housekeeper earlier that day had been vague at best. Perhaps intentionally so, Jack suspected.

As an experienced investigative journalist, Jack knew how to get access to people who didn't know him, and would perhaps prefer to leave it that way. Making contact with Bernard Lloyd had been a challenge. As Jack could spare only two days in Sydney before he had to return to the war zone in Afghanistan to continue his assignment, time was of the essence. However, Jack was determined to find out as much as he could about the little gold cross that appeared to be the only link to his birth mother.

As soon as he arrived home, Jack contacted a colleague who had successfully interviewed Lloyd a few years ago. What he found out wasn't encouraging. Lloyd lived like a monastic recluse on a remote property surrounded by a national park, two hours' drive south of Sydney. He rarely gave interviews, was virtually impossible to contact, and had famously said, 'The older I get, I like more and more people, less and less.'

'That just about sums it up,' his friend had told Jack. 'Lloyd's very difficult. The only way in is through his housekeeper, who is also his secretary. She guards him like a lioness guards her cubs. Good luck!' But as Jack was soon to find out, his friend hadn't told him everything, although he had given him a phone number.

The telephone conversation with the housekeeper earlier that day had been brief and to the point. Jack had decided the best way to approach his request to see Lloyd was to be totally honest. Realising there would be no second chances, he told the housekeeper about his father's recent death, his meeting with the pawnbroker, the significance of the little cross, and why he wanted to find out more about it. The housekeeper said she would talk to Lloyd and call back. Disappointed, Jack took this as a polite fob off. However, an hour later, the housekeeper did ring back and gave Jack directions to the remote property.

After fording several creeks, dodging rocks and fallen trees and almost getting bogged down on a steep slope, Jack reached a sunny clearing. As soon as he set eyes on the old homestead with its crooked chimney and corrugated iron roof and surrounded by tall eucalypts, Jack understood why an artist like Lloyd would want to live there. The natural bush setting was breathtaking. To Jack, it looked like something out of the gold rush days that Tom Roberts would like to have painted. With a fast-flowing creek blocking the end of the track ahead, the only way to the house was over a narrow wooden bridge.

Jack parked his SUV – by now covered in mud – and began to cross the bridge.

'You found it. Not many do,' a voice called out from somewhere in the trees. 'A good start.'

Jack stopped and turned around. First, he saw a horse's head appear from behind one of the trees, then a rider – a woman. The horse trotted towards the bridge and stopped. The woman jumped off and tied the horse to a bridge post. She took off her broad-brimmed hat and shook her head to loosen her white-blonde hair, glistening in the morning sun like the silk of a shogun's kimono.

'I'm Ingrid,' said the woman, extending her hand. 'We spoke earlier.'

Jack looked at the striking, confident woman smiling at him. Tall and slim, in her fifties, immaculately dressed in riding boots, moleskins and a checked shirt, she looked more like someone going to a gymkhana than the housekeeper of an eccentric old painter with a fearsome reputation.

'Not the dragon you expected, I can see,' said the woman, laughing. 'I get this all the time.'

Jack smiled, but didn't reply.

'I saw you crossing the creek further down the track and was hoping to make it back before you arrived. I ride every morning. Come, let me introduce you to my husband.'

The sundrenched, barn-like studio with its floor-to-ceiling windows at the back of the homestead overlooked a billabong and the dense bush beyond. Lloyd stood in front of a large canvas, his hands covered in paint. Small pieces of discarded rags, open tins and empty tubes of paint littered the wooden floor.

'I start work very early,' said Lloyd. 'That's when the light is at its best. Light is everything.' Lloyd applied some blue paint with his thumb, wiped his hand with a cloth, which he then dropped on the floor, and turned to face Jack. 'Painting is a passion; an all-consuming one. Sleep is a necessity I would like to do without, but can't. Well, not entirely. At my age, every hour counts.'

Barefoot, his long white hair pulled back and tied in a ponytail and wearing a loose Hawaiian shirt over baggy shorts covered in paint, Lloyd looked at Jack with corn-blue eyes that seemed to belong to a much younger man, not one close to eighty.

'Are you a passionate man, Mr Rogan?'

'I suppose I am,' replied Jack, a little taken aback by the unexpected question.

'I hear your father died just the other day. I'm sorry. I remember when my father died; it's etched in my memory. Everything changed that day. The way I felt, the way I saw the world, the way I painted – everything. I grew up that day,' Lloyd paused and looked dreamily out of the window.

'Thank you for seeing me,' said Jack.

'Don't thank me; thank my wife. It was Ingrid who persuaded me to see you. Ingrid, and your articles.'

'My articles? In what way?' asked Jack, startled.

'I've read your *Voices from the Front Line*. You are not merely an observer, you are an *interpreter*. You show your readers what you see through the lens of compassion; humanity; grief. A painter does the same. That's why I wanted to meet you.'

'No-one has told me this before.'

Lloyd smiled and walked over to his wife standing by the door. 'Would you make us some tea, darling?' he said and kissed his wife tenderly on the cheek. Then he turned to Jack and shook his hand. 'It's a pleasure to meet you.'

'And you,' said Jack, enjoying the company of this fascinating man who seemed to fill the large room with his presence and his art.

'You are going back to Afghanistan?'

'Yes, tomorrow.'

'That's why the urgency; I understand.'

Jack nodded.

Lloyd pointed to his painting. 'Come, have a look at this. What do you see?'

Jack looked at the canvas, brimming with colour and unusual, abstract shapes. In essence, Lloyd was a landscape painter; all his paintings were inspired by the Australian bush. However, unlike other well-known Australian landscape painters like Arthur Streeton, Russell Drysdale, Frederick McCubbin and Sidney Nolan, who painted what they *saw*, Lloyd painted what he *felt*. That was his genius and what made his art so appealing and unique.

'What do I see?' said Jack shortly, taking a step back. 'I see the morning dew glistening on the bark of the ghost gums and leaves moving gently in the breeze. I see fern fronds meeting the morning sun and gnarled branches covered in fungi rotting on the forest floor, providing food for generations of insects and nourishing the cycle of life.'

Lloyd looked at Jack, taken aback. 'You put my shapes and colours into words. I wish my critics could do the same. Come, let's have some tea.'

'That's about it,' said Jack, sitting back in the awkward-looking, yet surprisingly comfortable chair constructed entirely of twisted branches and tree roots. He had told Lloyd and his wife all he knew about the little cross and his recent encounter with the bird-loving pawnbroker in Brisbane.

'I remember that chap,' said Lloyd, laughing. 'He was a little weird even then. I met him through a friend of mine, a doctor I went to school with. I lived in the Glasshouse Mountains not far from Brisbane at the time.'

Lloyd broke off, and poured Jack another cup of tea.

'He told me he had this patient – a pawnbroker – who boasted about a fabulous little gold cross, an original Fabergé from Paris that he had for sale in his shop,' continued Lloyd. 'It was stunning. I fell in love with it as soon as I saw it. Ingrid was expecting our first child at the time, so I went to see the pawnbroker and bought the cross for her as a present. That's all there is to it, really.'

'Do you still have it?' asked Jack hopefully, leaning forward.

'In a way, yes,' replied Ingrid. 'I gave it to our daughter when she left home a few years ago and went to America—'

'Chasing a dream,' interrupted Lloyd, the sadness in his voice obvious.

'What kind of dream?'

'She's a jazz singer,' said Ingrid, a sparkle in her eyes. 'A rather good one.'

'Really?' said Jack, surprised. 'What's her name?'

'Her name's Rachael, but she goes under the name of *Soul*.'

'*What?*' said Jack, almost dropping his cup. 'Soul is your daughter?'

Ingrid beamed like only a proud mother can, and nodded.

Soul – a tall, leggy blonde with a voice like the legendary Etta James – was a music sensation. Her promotional videos were legendary, and her concerts were sold out months in advance.

'Wow! Where does she live now?'

'She's based in New York, but tours a lot. I can give you her number if you like. I'm sure she would be happy to meet you and show you the little cross, if that's what you would like. It's her good luck charm. She never takes it off.'

'I would love that,' said Jack. 'Thank you so much.'

'We speak on Skype several times a week,' continued Ingrid and stood up. 'I'll tell her about you next time she calls.'

Jack stood up as well. 'Thank you again,' he said, shaking his head. 'Soul is your daughter; amazing!'

Ingrid accompanied Jack back to his car. 'If you do get to see my daughter,' she said just before Jack closed the door, 'please call me. My number's on the piece of paper I gave you. I'm worried about her—'

'Why?'

'Fame can be very intoxicating, especially for someone so young. I can't leave here and travel,' Ingrid continued, lowering her voice, 'I'm sure you understand.'

'Perfectly.'

'I knew you would.'

As Jack looked at the striking woman standing next to him, he could sense anguish and pain. 'Is there anything in particular that concerns you?' he asked.

'Yes.'

'What is it?'

'Bad company, and drugs.'

THE POKER GAME

Jack finished his second gin and tonic, took a deep breath and let himself sink into the comfortable Qantas business class seat. *Nine hours to Singapore*, he thought. *Bliss ... before the nightmare starts again.* Jack was on his way back to the frontline in Afghanistan to continue his assignment. This was his first bit of quiet-time since his father's funeral. Feeling relaxed and sleepy, he closed his eyes and listened to the mesmerising hum of the engines.

He had just finished reading the articles Maud had copied for him in Brisbane, trying to make some sense of the sensational murder trial that had caused so much interest and ignited such passion in Perth in 1970. A fatal stabbing in a dark alley in Broome was hardly the stuff to warrant more than a few lines in the paper's court report. However, this particular case had the whole of Perth in its grip and had sent ripples of curiosity and fascination across the whole of Australia.

The public couldn't get enough of it and followed the proceedings day by day, witness by witness, as the trial unfolded in the Supreme Court. The articles reported the evidence of all the colourful key witnesses in great detail, almost like a transcript. And it was all due to one thing: a pearl. Not just any pearl, but the legendary Kimberley Queen, the biggest pearl ever found in Australia.

Jack let his mind wander as he tried to tie together the fragmented pieces of evidence into some coherent, chronological order, until a certain picture emerged of that fateful day in Broome. Unfortunately, the picture was incomplete and there were many frustrating gaps. It had all begun with a poker game in the notorious Roebuck Hotel on 22 November 1969 ...

* * *

Saturday night at the Roebuck Hotel was always a rowdy affair. The Roey, as it was affectionately called by the locals, was a much-loved Broome institution. Established in 1880 to provide some entertainment for the boisterous pearl lugger crews after a long, dangerous season at sea, The Roey had been a popular watering hole for generations of pearlers and outback adventurers.

The wet season had started early that year and the relentless rain, oppressive heat and almost unbearable humidity had everyone on edge. The ships had returned to shore, the pearl divers had stopped diving, and many had left town and gone south until the next season started in April. There were hardly any tourists about and most operators had closed shop. Those who had decided to stay behind flocked to the only place of amusement: the pub. And in the pub there wasn't much more one could do than have a few beers with mates and gamble. Or, have a few beers and watch others gamble.

A big poker game was in full swing at one of the tables in the back of the bar. The stakes had reached dizzying heights, driven by huge egos, rivalry and booze. Curious onlookers crowded around the table – ten deep – watching the game.

Bryn Evans appeared to be on an uncanny winning streak. The game that had started two hours ago with six players, now had only four left. Licking their wounds caused by huge losses, two had left the table and had joined the ranks of the spectators. As every experienced poker player knows, trying to win back losses can quickly become fatal. However, that didn't seem to deter Andy Morgan, who was by now gambling recklessly. With several thousand dollars in the pot, the game was quickly spinning out of control.

The rivalry between Bryn and Andy went back many years. Both were outstanding pearl divers, and both held records. But Andy had one big advantage: he was the son of one of the wealthiest and most powerful cultured pearl farmers in Broome. His family had been involved in pearling since well before the First World War. Bryn, on the other hand, had arrived in Broome as a penniless teenager from Wales. He had worked his way up the risky and dangerous pearling ladder until he had been able to establish his own small cultured pearl farming business in Cygnet Bay a few years earlier.

The business was hugely successful from the very start, due mainly to Bryn's diving skills and intimate knowledge of the rich pearl shell beds off the Kimberley coast. To that, he had recently added another rare and much sought after skill without which pearl farming wasn't possible: he travelled regularly to Japan during the wet seasons to learn the difficult but necessary know-how to operate and implant nuclei into pearl oysters.

It was after Bryn had won again that Andy did something extraordinary – and reckless. While playing the next hand, he put his cards face down on the table and announced he wanted to raise the stakes. Having run out of cash, he took something out of his waistcoat pocket and placed it on the table in front of him. The spectators gasped as soon as they realised what it was. It was the legendary Kimberley Queen, the biggest pearl ever found in Australian waters. The pearl was priceless and had been in the Morgan family since it was discovered in 1904 by a Japanese diver working for the Morgans on one of their pearl luggers. It weighed 102 grains and was the size of a sparrow's egg, with a lustre so alluring it would have beguiled even the most discerning maharaja.

Andy, by now heavily intoxicated, looked at Bryn sitting opposite. 'How about it, mate?' he said, his speech slurred. 'Have you got the balls to put your precious little pearling business on the table?' He reached for the pearl in front of him and held it up. 'I reckon this little beauty's worth as much, if not a lot more. What do you say?'

Excitement rippled through the stunned spectators, mesmerised by the epic showdown unfolding in front of them. For a while, Bryn looked at his cards in silence, his mind racing, and then nodded. 'You're on. But I strongly advise you against putting up the Kimberley Queen. Your dad ...'

'Who the fuck do you think you are?' growled Andy, almost choking with anger. 'You don't tell me what to do!'

Bryn and Andy had been close friends for a long time, until something – or rather someone – had come between them a few years earlier that had destroyed their friendship: a woman. Andy had met her in Paris during one of his wet season Europe trips. The stunning young woman had returned with him to Broome. That's how she met Bryn...

Bryn shrugged. 'Have it your way,' he said, and looked again at his cards.

* * *

During the stopover in Singapore, Jack, a methodical man, pieced together a rough outline of the extraordinary court case and jotted down some key points in the little notebook he always carried in his back pocket. It was the way he approached every assignment. After peeling away all the commentary, speculation and sensational bits, he had to admit that the story was incomplete at best. One of the main aspects of the case that interested him most – Bryn the man, and his character and personality – had been almost completely ignored. If it should turn out that this man was in fact his biological father, then Jack wanted to know a lot more about him, and what had happened to him.

To Jack, there appeared to be only one way he could possibly do this successfully after all these years: speak to someone who knew Bryn at the time, and was with him during this difficult period. Jack drew a circle around a name he had jotted down earlier: Jeremy Ellicott QC, the barrister who had defended Bryn at his trial.

The Judge in Perth: 25 March 2002

Jack spent another exhausting week in the Shai-Kot Valley in Afghanistan. As Gurrul had correctly predicted, his father's death and extraordinary deathbed revelations had affected Jack deeply. Suddenly, the past looked like quicksand and Jack's whole identity was under a cloud of uncertainty.

Bryn's trial and unanswered questions haunted Jack during the few hours of restless sleep he managed to snatch between bloody Taliban ambushes and coalition counter-attacks. However, despite all this, he made some progress. To begin with, he found out that Jeremy Ellicott QC was now Justice Ellicott, a Supreme Court judge in Perth.

Jack knew it was time to get away from the war for a while; take a break to reflect and put everything into some kind of perspective. He also knew that he wouldn't be able to do that until he had some answers to the burning questions that were troubling him. Once again, Jack contacted a friend – an editor at one of Perth's leading newspapers he had known for years – and asked him for a favour. In Jack's line of work, connections were everything, and favours were the way to tackle difficult matters. And nothing could have been more difficult than to get access to Justice Ellicott at short notice. But that was precisely what his friend had been able to arrange.

Jack's flight from Bangkok had been delayed. That only gave him an hour to get from the airport to the Supreme Court in the centre of Perth to keep his appointment with Justice Ellicott. Used to tight schedules and impossible deadlines, Jack jumped into a taxi and went straight to the court. A shower and a change of clothes would have to wait. Being late wasn't an option.

Jack made it to the associate's office with ten minutes to spare.

'I came straight from the airport,' he said, pointing apologetically to his luggage.

'Where did you fly in from?' asked the judge's associate, a young woman, sizing up Jack with interest.

'A war.'

The woman raised an eyebrow. 'I'll tell His Honour you're here.'

'You've been in a war, Mr Rogan? What kind of war?' said the judge – a distinguished-looking man in his late sixties – extending his hand.

'Shai-Kot Valley; Afghanistan. I was there less than twenty-four hours ago.'

'What were you doing there?' asked the judge, intrigued.

'I'm a war correspondent.'

'My son's in the army. He's currently serving in Afghanistan. Tell me, what was it like?'

Jack described the battle of Takur Ghar and mentioned his articles.

'What a coincidence,' said the judge. 'My son was there too.'

How fortuitous, thought Jack, smiling. After that, the conversation became more personal and relaxed.

'You have friends in high places, Mr Rogan,' continued the judge, changing the subject. 'The police commissioner told me you wanted to talk to me about Bryn Evans. I must say, I'm intrigued ... that was all such a long time ago. What's your interest in this?'

Jack had no idea what the judge was talking about. He certainly didn't know any police commissioner in Perth and put the curious remark down to something his friend must have somehow engineered, to open the door.

Jack decided to cut to the chase. 'I have reason to believe that Bryn Evans is my father.'

The judge looked at Jack in amazement, and nodded. 'I understand.

During the next hour, Jack found the answers to many of the questions that had troubled him, but not all. He found out that Bryn had left the Roebuck Hotel just before midnight with a lot of cash and the Kimberley Queen. After that, accounts differed as to what happened.

According to Bryn, on his way home he was attacked in China Lane by two men armed with knives. It was raining, and they demanded he hand over the Kimberley Queen. Bryn, a physically powerful man, told them to get lost and fought them off with a flick knife he always carried with him. During the altercation, he was attacked by a third man from behind. As he turned around to face the man, the man lunged at him out of the dark and Bryn stabbed him in the chest in an attempt to defend himself. Fatally wounded, the man fell to the ground. The man was Andy Morgan. Realising what had happened, the other two men fled.

However, there was another version:

The two men who, according to Bryn, attacked him and demanded he hand over the Kimberley Queen, told the police they overheard a heated argument between two men in China Lane. When they went to investigate, they saw Bryn stab a man in the chest and then run away.

'That's about it,' said the judge. 'The police found Andy Morgan lying dead in China Lane with a knife in his chest. The knife belonged to Bryn and had his fingerprints all over it. Bryn had fled the scene and couldn't be found. That was his biggest mistake and, I believe, the main reason the jury convicted him. They saw it as an admission of guilt. Bryn was apprehended two weeks later. The police located him with the help of Aboriginal trackers. He was hiding in a cave near the Kalumburu Mission in the Kimberley.'

'Did he explain why he fled?'

'Yes. He said, had he stayed with the body, he would certainly have been killed. He saw the two men who had attacked him earlier, return with others. Remember, the Morgans were one of the most powerful families in Broome at the time.'

'Has this been investigated?' asked Jack.

'Not really. The police viewed this as an open-and-shut case.'

'Not very professional, was it?'

The judge shrugged. 'You must remember, Broome thirty years ago wasn't what it is today. It was a very different place; rough, remote, dangerous. The police were under-resourced and inexperienced in dealing with a complex murder case. And the trial took place here in Perth, two thousand kilometres away. Locating witnesses and bringing them to Perth was almost impossible. No-one wanted to talk. No-one saw anything. No-one wanted to get involved. Outback mentality.'

'Could the Morgans have had something to do with this?'

'Quite possibly.'

'And the motive for the attack? Robbery, you think?'

'According to Bryn, Andy was in a rage after the game because he had lost the Kimberley Queen. Apparently, he was convinced Bryn had been cheating. Andy's father was a tyrant and a bully. Andy was terrified of his father and afraid of what he would do if he found out that his son had lost the Kimberley Queen in a poker game. Andy desperately wanted the pearl back – at any cost. Simple as that.'

'Was this raised at the trial?'

'We did our best to introduce this, but it wasn't easy. Lack of witnesses again. Speculation isn't evidence.'

As an experienced interviewer, Jack sensed a certain irritation in the judge's demeanour. He obviously didn't like the questions. Jack decided to change direction.

'What happened to Bryn?'

'He was found guilty of murder and sentenced to death. This was later commuted to life imprisonment. The death penalty wasn't abolished in Western Australia until 1984. Eric Cooke was the last man to be hanged in Fremantle Prison that same year. Bryn was sent to Fremantle Prison to serve his time.'

'But the prison was decommissioned in 1991. What happened to him after that?'

The judge looked at Jack – sadness in his eyes – and took a deep breath. 'He died during a prison riot in 1988. Didn't you know?'

'No. How did he die?'

'He burnt to death in his cell.'

'Oh my God! And the Kimberley Queen?'

'Has never been found.'

FREMANTLE PRISON: 26 MARCH 2002

Jack decided to stay in Perth for an extra day and visit the notorious Fremantle Prison – now a World Heritage Site open to the public – to see for himself where Bryn had died in such violent and tragic circumstances. He also wanted to find out more about the 1988 prison riot Justice Ellicott had told him about.

Jack caught the Swan River ferry from Perth to Fremantle, thinking about the prison's history that he had read in a brochure he'd picked up at the tourist information office the day before:

… The decision to build such a large prison in a distant, fledgling colony was entirely due to a major problem on the other side of the world. British jails and rotting prison hulks could no longer cope. The convict population was growing at an alarming rate and had to be accommodated somewhere, preferably faraway and out of sight. The solution? Western Australia.

In May 1850, Western Australia was declared a penal settlement by the British government and it was decided to send ten thousand convicts to the Antipodes. It soon became apparent that to make this possible, a large, new jail was needed. Planning and construction of 'The Establishment', as it was called at the time, began in 1852, and was completed in 1859. Built entirely by convicts who arrived from Britain in ever-increasing numbers, the construction of such a large prison complex – built of stone quarried nearby – was an extraordinary achievement, bearing in mind the primitive conditions, lack of skills and materials…

Rather than catch one of the tourist buses waiting at the terminal, Jack decided to walk up to the grim prison complex that had dominated the historic township for almost 150 years. Even now, years after it had been decommissioned and opened to the public, the imposing prison structure on the hill overlooking Fremantle was intimidating. Jack looked at the tall, grey stone walls and the massive front gate flanked by two arrogant towers. *A monolith of loneliness and pain*, he thought, remembering more of what he had read about the jail the night before:

... Hundreds of convicts locked in tiny cells, smaller than those of Britain's notorious Pentonville prison; brutal, bloody floggings where the flesh was torn off the backs of hapless, screaming men by the dreaded cat o'nine tails; harsh discipline and relentless, mind-numbing routine. Year, after year, after year. And then there was the ultimate punishment: death by hanging. Forty-six men and one woman died on the gallows inside the prison. Lives snuffed out by harsh laws without mercy and brutish executioners, their faces hidden behind leather masks ...

Jack bought a ticket and waited in the courtyard for the tour to begin. The elderly guide, a former warder, gave a brief history of the jail and then walked the visitors through the prisoner admission process before taking them into the main block.

The tour lasted for more than an hour. What made it so interesting for Jack – and so chilling – was the fact that the prison was totally intact. The only thing missing were the inmates. Their presence still lingered, though. Everywhere. It reminded Jack of his visit to Auschwitz, where the ghosts of an unspeakable past were never far away.

Towards the end of the tour, the guide finally broached the subject Jack had been waiting for: the 1988 riot.

'Over here, ladies and gentlemen,' began the warder, pointing to an open prison cell, 'is one of the most infamous cells in the entire prison. It belonged to a notorious prisoner – a lifer. His name was Bryn Evans, a convicted murderer. What makes this cell so special is the stunning murals on the walls. Bryn Evans taught himself to paint here in prison and became an accomplished artist. He painted many murals in the exercise yards, depicting prison life. Unfortunately, those murals have long gone. But the ones in his cell here survived even the riot of 1988 and the fire that killed him. You can go inside and take photographs.'

Jack was one of the last to go into the tiny cell. Choking with emotion, he carefully photographed all the murals before stepping outside to join the others.

'Christmas of 1987 had been incredibly hot,' continued the guide. 'For days, the temperature reached forty degrees or more in the shade. The conditions in the cells were unbearable, the exercise yards had turned into ovens, and tempers had reached breaking point. Then, during the afternoon of 4 January 1988, the place erupted. I was there ...'

* * *

Prison Officer Brian Todd was on patrol in number three division. All was quiet. He looked at his watch, went to the phone and called a colleague in another division. Officer Todd was unaware that a group of prisoners was watching him carefully. Before he could put down the phone, someone shouted, '*Now!*'

The fuse had been lit.

Officer Todd was the first warder to be overpowered. Within moments, prisoners armed with pieces of furniture, buckets, broken plates, anything, ran along the landings, attacking officers and herding them into an exercise yard as hostages.

Intensified by the unbearable heat and years of frustration, bottled-up grievances exploded into a frenzy of violence and feverish action as the prisoners ran amok, attacking guards and lighting fires in the cells.

'All right, lads, we've been waiting a long time for this,' said Joe O'Reilly, a notorious prisoner known for his violent temper. O'Reilly, a huge, broad-shouldered man, regularly spent time in solitary, which had earned him the nickname 'Lonely Joe'.

'Can you see him?' asked one of Lonely Joe's accomplices, a young man with a scar running down one cheek, a souvenir from a fatal pub brawl that had landed him in jail.

'No, he must still be in his cell. Perfect. Let's pay the cocky bastard a visit,' said Lonely Joe, laughing.

Bryn was sitting on his bunk listening to the commotion outside, when three men burst into his tiny cell. Lonely Joe grabbed Bryn by the collar, pulled him up and pushed him against the wall, his sweaty face glowing with excitement. Taken by surprise and with no room to move, Bryn was unable to put up any resistance, or push his attacker aside.

'Now listen carefully, you Welsh prick,' hissed Lonely Joe, his evil-smelling breath tickling Bryn's nose. 'I've been dying to ask you this for years ...'

The two accomplices laughed.

'Everyone knows you hid the Kimberley Queen somewhere in the bush before the coppers got you. It's out there somewhere and you know where it is, right?'

'I do, you stupid Irish moron,' replied Bryn calmly. 'Now piss off!'

Lonely Joe stared at Bryn, astonished. It wasn't the response he had expected. Overcome by anger, he clenched his fists and took a tiny step back. Before he could punch Bryn in the stomach, Bryn headbutted him, splitting his forehead open. Dazed, Lonely Joe lost his balance and fell backwards onto the bunk behind him. Bryn was about to finish him off, when the two accomplices jumped into action and pinned Bryn against the wall. Lonely Joe wiped away the blood trickling down his face and into his eyes and stood up. 'You asked for it, you piece of shit,' he said and began to punch Bryn, first in the stomach and then in the face, the massive blows breaking Bryn's jaw and nose, and drawing blood almost immediately.

'That's enough, mate!' said one of the accomplices holding Bryn. 'You'll kill the bastard. Then what?'

'You're right,' said Lonely Joe, massaging his knuckles. 'Let's continue our little chat. Where's the Kimberley Queen?'

'You really expect me to tell you? You're obviously dumber than you look,' said Bryn, spitting out a bloody tooth.

That's when Lonely Joe lost it. In a rage and oblivious to the smoke drifting into the cell and the commotion and shouting outside, he began to hoe into Bryn like a man possessed, until Bryn's body went limp. The two accomplices let go. Covered in blood, Bryn slid to the floor, lifeless as a sack of potatoes.

'Shit! We better get out of here,' shouted one of the men and headed for the cell door. The other did the same. Lonely Joe gave Bryn a hefty farewell kick in the back, and then followed his mates outside and closed the cell door behind him.

Outside it was bedlam. The prisoners had set many of the cells on fire, which then rapidly spread to the dry timber roof beams above. Soon, the entire block was ablaze with smoke billowing from windows like dragon's breath, alerting Fremantle to serious trouble at the jail.

Choking on the acrid, deadly smoke filling the cell, Bryn opened his eyes and tried in vain to pull himself up. His whole body felt numb. In a daze and haemorrhaging internally, he began to cough as blood filled his lungs. With fading eyesight, Bryn looked at the small mural in front of him. It was the last one in a series of twelve, depicting striking cliffs, boab trees, picturesque bays, waterfalls and ancient Aboriginal cave art he had visited in the remote Kimberley he loved so much. They were precious little windows into his previous life; reminders of freedom.

Bryn managed a crooked smile as he looked at the panel and remembered O'Reilly's question: *'Where's the Kimberley Queen?'* With the last of his remaining strength, Bryn reached across to the mural – his hand shaking and covered in blood – and pressed the bloody tips of his fingers against a certain rock in the picture, like a signature or gesture of farewell. Moments later, Bryn drifted into the cottonwool-bliss of unconsciousness as his lungs filled with more smoke and blood, slowly shutting down his brain.

* * *

'The riot lasted well into the night,' continued the guide, 'with fifteen warders held in the exercise yard like frightened cattle awaiting their fate. By now, the roof had collapsed and flames lit up the night sky. Negotiations with the ringleaders failed and the police surrounded the prison to prevent a mass escape.'

'How was this resolved?' asked someone in the tour.

'Dressed in riot gear and armed with batons, prison officers stormed the jail shortly after midnight, but to no avail. The rioters wouldn't surrender, nor did they release their hostages. The stand-off lasted for nineteen hours until the rioters finally capitulated and released the last of the hostages. The crisis was over. This dreadful incident and the lengthy trial of the thirty-three prisoners charged marked the beginning of the end of the prison. It was decommissioned in 1991.'

Jack fell in beside the guide on the way back to the entrance. 'How did Bryn Evans die?' he asked.

'We found him lying on the floor in his cell, dead and badly burnt. He had been trapped by the fire.'

'His murals weren't damaged?'

'Apart from some bloodstains on one of the murals, surprisingly, no.' said the guard, lowering his voice. 'It was decided to leave the stains untouched, so as not to damage the artwork. It's a tourist attraction.'

Jack stopped and called up the photos of the murals on his camera. 'Please show me,' he said. 'Which one has the bloodstains?'

The guard pointed to one of the murals. 'That one there, the last one right at the bottom near the door. We don't talk about it during the tour. A little too gruesome even for a place like this, don't you think?'

'A dead man's blood left on …?' Jack shrugged, thanked the guide and headed for the gates, glad to leave the place that had witnessed so much misery and pain.

THE JAZZ SINGER IN NEW YORK: MORNING, 30 MARCH 2002

Jack had hoped that after talking to the judge and his visit to Fremantle Prison, he would be able to relax a little and put the disturbing matter of his father's astonishing deathbed revelation out of his mind at least for a little while, to enjoy some time with friends at home before he had to return to the war in Afghanistan. However, the more he tried to banish the uncertainty, the nagging doubts and unanswered questions, the stronger they became, until finally defeated Jack decided to use the remaining few days of his self-imposed leave to continue his investigation.

Having exhausted his lead into Bryn Evans and his tragic story, Jack turned to something he hoped would be more promising: the little Fabergé gold cross. Perhaps it would give up some of its secrets and shed some light on the mystery surrounding his birth and adoption.

A visit to one of Jack's newspaper contacts in New York was definitely overdue. A trip to the Big Apple was therefore warranted and made sense. At the same time, Jack was planning to somehow make contact with Lloyd's daughter, Soul, the famous jazz singer. She was giving a concert in the Beacon Theatre in New York on the weekend as part of her *A Tribute to Etta James's Tour*, and Jack was hoping to somehow procure a ticket and meet her. A long shot for sure, he had to admit, but definitely worth a try.

Jack arrived in New York on Friday and checked into a modest hotel in the Bronx he had used before. The Soul concert was completely booked out, and his chances of obtaining a ticket the day before the event looked bleak. As a last resort, Jack decided to call the telephone number Ingrid Lloyd had given him, to try to make contact with Soul personally. He did so reluctantly because he was afraid of what would happen if the phone call failed to deliver.

On Saturday morning – jetlagged and with no hope of obtaining a ticket – Jack made the call. A man answered. Taken aback, Jack identified himself as a family friend from Australia with an important message from Soul's mother. After an agonising silence the man said, 'Wait a moment; she's just stepping out of the shower.'

Great! Just my luck. She'll be pissed off for sure, thought Jack, feeling more anxious by the second.

Then a voice came on the line; soft, warm and friendly. 'A message from my mother? How intriguing ...'

'I wish I could hand you a towel first, to make this a little easier for both of us,' was all Jack managed to say.

'Are you spying on me?' said Soul, laughing. '*Who are you?*'

'Jack Rogan. I visited your parents a couple of weeks ago.'

'Ah. The man from the war. Mum spoke about you the other day. You must have made quite an impression.'

'Story of my life.'

'What can I do for you?'

'I flew in last night and tried to get a ticket for this evening's concert.'

'Good luck!'

'Exactly.'

'Are you a fan?'

'Not yet. I was hoping to find out though, and somehow meet you after the concert to—'

'Talk about my little gold cross?'

'My goodness, news travels fast.'

'So, why not do both?'

'What do you mean?'

'Well, you could come to the concert and find out if you are perhaps a potential fan, and we could meet afterwards and talk about the little cross.'

'But—'

'I know, you have no ticket,' interrupted Soul, enjoying the banter. 'No problem. One will be waiting for you at the entrance.'

'Thank you,' stammered Jack, 'you are most—'

'Must dash. My manager keeps staring at me, and the puddle on the floor is growing at an alarming rate.'

'Sorry.'

'Don't be. Hope you like my music.'

Then the phone went dead.

Slowly, Jack put down the receiver. Did this really happen? *he asked himself, shaking his head.* Have I just spoken to a superstar and arranged a date?

The Beacon Theatre on 2124 Broadway with its sparkling Roaring Twenties art deco grandeur and intimate setting had been a popular New York institution since it opened its doors in 1929. Over the years, it had seen some of the greatest names in music perform under its roof, and hosted many of the most memorable events in the must-do calendar of the social elite.

Jack arrived early, collected his ticket and watched the New York glitterati pull up in their chauffeur-driven limousines. Impressed, Jack recognised many famous faces and thanked his lucky stars to have such a prized ticket in his coat pocket.

Soon after the first bell, and with a tingle of excitement, Jack followed the crowd inside and took his seat right in the centre of the Lodge, with an uninterrupted view of the stage. *Not bad for a boy from the bush, as Gurrul would say,* thought Jack as the lights dimmed, raising the spine-tingling atmosphere of anticipation another notch.

For a few tense seconds there was total silence as the curtains parted, and then the band began to play a medley of Etta James's greatest hits. Then a circle of light appeared on the floor of the dark stage like a searching finger, and a voice drifted out of somewhere in the darkness. Softly at first, but becoming stronger with each haunting phrase. It was almost instantly drowned out by enthusiastic applause, preparing the way for the adored star to make her appearance.

As every diva knows, the entry is critically important, and sets the tone for the entire performance.

Dressed in an elegant, figure-hugging black gown by Dior – a perfect contrast to her long, luxurious white-blonde hair swishing across her exposed shoulders – Soul stepped into the circle of light and delivered an emotional rendition of Etta James's iconic song – *At Last* – which had the audience spellbound. Her diction, timing and delivery were perfect, but Soul added her own distinctive style that gave the familiar song its own 'Soul-charm'. It wasn't an imitation, rather an *interpretation* of the much-loved lyrics, by a remarkable young artist in her twenties displaying the maturity of someone twice her age.

Amazing. She sounds just like Etta, thought Jack as he tried to make out if the sparkling piece of jewellery around Soul's neck was in fact the little cross she supposedly never took off.

After that, Soul, an accomplished pianist, took a seat at the piano and sang several of her own songs before returning to another Etta James's classic that brought the house down.

At the beginning of the interval, an usher walked up to Jack. 'Soul would like to meet you, sir. Please, come with me.'

Surprised, Jack followed the usher backstage.

Soul sat on a stool in front of a large ornate mirror, a glass of champagne in her hand. Her hairdresser stood next to her and was adjusting her hair. Jack saw Soul looking at him in the mirror. For an instant, their eyes locked, then Soul turned around.

'Ah. A new fan perhaps, or is it too early to tell?'

Jack put on a serious face. 'Hm … not quite sure yet, only kidding! You have an amazing voice.' *She looks just like her mother*, thought Jack. *Even the voice …*

Green eyes, thought Soul, watching Jack with interest. *No wonder Mum thought he was a dish.* 'So, what's this important message from my mother?' she asked, a sparkle in her eyes.

'She says hello.'

'Is that it?'

Looking sheepish, Jack nodded. 'I exaggerated. Just a little …'

Soul burst out laughing. 'No lecture to deliver; no warning to convey?'

'You are twisting the knife!'

'Champagne?'

'That would help.'

'Help? In what way?'

'Make me feel a little less embarrassed. And it would definitely help me to stop staring at the little cross you are wearing around your neck.'

Soul touched the exquisite little cross with the tips of her fingers. 'Of course; that's why you're here. Mum told me the story—'

'There's more ...'

Soul's manager – a short, portly man – burst into the room, and looked disapprovingly at Jack. 'Ten minutes!' he said to Soul. 'Better get ready.'

Soul turned towards the mirror. 'Yes, David,' she said and winked at Jack. 'He drives me nuts!' she continued, lowering her voice. 'Champagne will have to wait, I'm afraid.'

'I better go,' said Jack.

'We are having a few drinks at my place after the concert. Why don't you come along and join us? David will give you the address.'

'Love to.'

'Remember, only fans are allowed,' teased Soul.

'I'm well on the way.'

'I hope so.'

THE PARTY IN MANHATTAN:
AFTERNOON, 30 MARCH 2002

After the concert, Jack caught a taxi back to his hotel to collect his camera before going to Soul's apartment. He was hoping to take a few close-ups of the little cross and look for possible clues that might help him trace its original owner.

Located close to the Metropolitan Museum of Art, the penthouse on top of an elegant, nineteen forties building occupied an entire floor. By the time Jack arrived, the party was already in full swing. Soft music, subdued lighting and floor-to-ceiling windows overlooking Central Park gave the apartment a movie-like ambience, oozing money and class.

Classic Manhattan, thought Jack. A waitress offered him a drink as soon as he stepped out of the lift and for a while Jack stood in the shadows, watching.

There was something distinctly odd about the people. At first, Jack couldn't quite work out what it was, but then it struck him: there were virtually no men in the room. The room was full of women. Women were dancing with each other in groups of three or four, kissing and moving in slow motion. Women were embracing on lounges or sitting on the floor. Some of them were outrageously dressed, others – with arms and even necks heavily tattooed – were barely dressed at all, exposed flesh promising excitement and danger. But they all seemed to have one thing in common: they appeared to be floating in their own, separate world, making Jack feel like an intruder looking in from the outside, like a voyeur.

A young woman walked up to Jack and stared at him with glassy eyes, her heavy make-up and puffy 'trout-pout' giving her an almost theatrical look. 'Want some?' she asked. 'There's plenty over there.' She pointed to a pair of young women sitting on a couch. They were giggling and holding something to their noses. *Snorting coke, I bet*, thought Jack, shaking his head. *Drugs everywhere.*

'Suit yourself, jerk,' said the woman and walked away.

Feeling out of place, Jack was about to put down his glass when he heard a soft voice call out from behind.

'What kept you? I thought you must have changed your mind.'

Jack spun around and looked at Soul standing behind him. Dressed in a stunning, impossibly tight bodysuit covered in silver beads, which left little to the imagination, Soul smiled at Jack.

'Not quite your scene, is it?' she said.

'It's different.'

'My world *is* different, and so are my friends. Inspiration for my songs comes in many forms—'

'And at a price,' Jack cut in.

Soul looked at Jack dreamily and took him by the hand. 'Come, Jack, let me introduce you to a special friend of mine.'

'What do I call you – *Soul*?'

'Out there on the stage I'm Soul. In here, I'm Rachael. That's what my friends call me; come.'

She's on drugs, thought Jack, recognising tell-tale signs of cocaine use: effusive enthusiasm; disinhibition; changes in concentration and focus.

'Several angels are here tonight,' continued Soul, guiding Jack unsteadily across the crowded room.

'Angels?'

'Victoria's Secret Angels ... You have heard of them, surely?' said Soul, lowering her voice.

'Leggy catwalk divas with strap-on wings and diamond-encrusted bikinis?'

'Very good. Here's one of them. Let me introduce you.'

Soul walked up to a stunning brunette and put her arm around her waist. The woman turned around, embraced Soul and kissed her passionately on the mouth.

'This is my dear friend Izabel from Brazil,' said Soul, her speech slurred, and took another drink from a passing waitress.

Cocaine and booze ... lethal, *thought Jack.*

Wearing black fishnet stockings, a tiny, sparkling bikini that showed off her amazing figure, and stilettos that looked like needles of glass, the breathtaking woman turned towards Jack.

'A man? How refreshing,' said Izabel, squeezing Jack's arm. 'Are you gay?'

'No. Will I be thrown out now?'

'Far from it. This lot here will eat you alive if you're not careful; trust me.'

'You can close your mouth now, Jack,' said Soul, laughing. 'Izabel is coming on tour with me. We start at the Paramount Theatre in Charlottesville, Virginia, followed by the Ohio Theatre in Columbus, and then the Louisville Palace in Louisville, Kentucky, or is it the other way 'round? Not quite sure of the order, but I'm performing in all these places. We are leaving in a couple of days. She's my lover. Are you shocked?'

'Not really.'

'Liar,' said Soul, leaning against Jack to steady herself. 'I can see it in your eyes.'

'Perhaps just a little.'

'That's much better. You should have come earlier. We could have had a chat then. It's too late now.'

'Sure.' Jack realised this certainly wasn't the time to talk about a piece of jewellery and take photographs. The entire subject now appeared pathetically trivial in a room full of decadence and excess. He also realised that staying would be a big mistake that he would regret in the morning. 'I think I better go. Long flight; jetlag,' he said, shrugging apologetically.

'A voice of reason; I understand. Tell you what,' said Soul, trying to focus. 'I jog every morning in the park. Why don't you join me and we can have a chat then? We could have some breakfast together.'

'Sounds great.'

'Do you know the Gapstow Bridge?'

'I do – 62nd Street, near the Pond.'

'One of my favourite spots in Central Park. Let's say eight, on the bridge?'

'You're on.'

'You're a breath of fresh air, Jack,' said Soul and kissed Jack on the cheek. 'A little sanity from Down Under. I desperately need a hand-brake, but not tonight.' Then she turned towards her leggy Brazilian friend, watching her intently. 'Izabel, darling, let's dance,' said Soul, kicking off her shoes.

The Incident in Central Park:
31 March 2002

Jack, an early riser, decided to walk rather than catch a cab to 62nd Street. He had mixed feelings about his rendezvous with Soul on the Gapstow Bridge in Central Park. But he knew the walk would do him good and help him put the turbulent events of the night before into proper context.

Troubled by the obvious drug-taking he had observed at the party, Jack had no doubt that Soul was heading for serious problems, perhaps even disaster. She had displayed all the classic symptoms of a habitual user; well beyond occasional, recreational dabbling with the alluring white poison that was so endemic in her circles.

Jack had come across serious, even fatal, drug use before. It was widespread among the armed forces in Afghanistan, and Jack had written about the devastating consequences of drug use in his *Voices from the Front Line*. One of his articles – *Drugs in the Firing Line* – had even won an award.

As Jack approached the picturesque little stone bridge he had photographed many times before, he could see the New York City skyline rising above the treetops. Illuminated by the morning sun, the breathtaking skyscrapers looked like arrogant beacons of man's dreams and ambitions, reaching for the stars.

Jack had grave doubts whether Soul would remember the arrangements they had made the night before, or even if she did, that she would actually turn up. Everything looks different in the morning, especially after a long night of excess. The cocktail of drugs and alcohol was bound to have taken its toll, and Jack knew jogging in Central Park in the morning might not seem so attractive in the harsh light of a new, sobering day.

Apart from a few early morning joggers and young, power-walking parents pushing designer prams, the park wasn't busy yet. The tourist invasion would come later.

Jack walked halfway across the little bridge and stopped to take in the view. He was about to reach for his camera when he noticed two tall women come jogging towards him. *Be buggered; it's them*, he thought and took a series of snapshots of the women as they approached. Dressed in activewear, their hair tucked under Nike baseball caps and wearing dark glasses, Soul and Izabel looked just like all the other women jogging through the park. No-one would have suspected that one of them was a celebrated superstar and the other a stunning Victoria's Secret Angel adored by millions.

Jack waved and was adjusting the zoom for a close-up when he saw one of the women stumble and then fall to the ground. It was Soul. Jack ran over to help. By the time he had covered the thirty or so metres, Izabel was kneeling on the pavement next to Soul with a worried look on her face, shaking her by the shoulders and pleading, 'Rachael, talk to me. Wake up!'

Jack looked at Soul lying on the ground – perfectly still – and didn't like what he saw. He quickly knelt down next to her and brought his face close to hers, almost touching the little cross. 'Rachael?' he said. Her eyes were closed, mouth open. *She isn't breathing.* He put his fingers to her wrist and checked her pulse. Nothing. *Heart attack,* thought Jack, a wave of panic rushing through him. *Jesus, she's gone into cardiac arrest!*

'Wh-what's wrong with her?' stammered Izabel, close to tears.

'Heart attack. Call an ambulance – now! Quickly!'

'Oh my God!'

Jack took off his sweater, pushed it under Soul's head and, taking a deep breath to calm himself, began to administer CPR by first methodically compressing her chest, and then exhaling air into her mouth to keep up the blood supply to the brain to avoid severe damage, or worse. Jack had seen CPR performed many times at the front, and knew exactly what to do. Like most journalists working in Afghanistan, he had also received basic CPR training.

Jack knew the next few minutes were critical. Life was hanging in the balance and major, permanent damage was a real possibility. He also realised this was most likely a drug-related episode, heart attack risk being higher after cocaine use. When combined with alcohol, it was even more dangerous.

By now, several people had gathered around, watching.

'Someone call an ambulance; *now*!' shouted Jack again, his voice sounding shrill.

'Already done,' said someone in the crowd. 'It's on its way.'

Feeling calmer, Jack continued. 'One, two, three, four, five,' he whispered, compressing Soul's chest. 'Stay with me.' Jack was beginning to sweat, his own heart racing as he continued the life-saving procedure.

After what seemed an eternity, the paramedics arrived. 'We'll take it from here, sir,' Jack heard someone say. Then he was pulled gently to his feet and taken aside. 'They know what to do,' said a young woman in uniform. 'You've done your part.'

Jack sat next to Izabel in the ambulance. She was crying and shaking uncontrollably. Jack could hear one of the paramedics speaking to the hospital on the radio; reporting in and giving instructions. Jack couldn't understand exactly what was being said because the siren was so loud, but he did catch that Soul's heart had been successfully restarted. *Thank God*, thought Jack, and put his arm around Izabel.

'She'll be all right,' he said, trying to comfort her.

'Y-you think so?' she stammered, unable to stop shaking.

'I do.'

After that, Izabel began mumbling softly in Portuguese. She was obviously praying. Moments later, the ambulance stopped, the doors were opened from the outside and the hospital team standing by took over.

Jack and Izabel sat in the hospital waiting room, anxiously waiting for news. Izabel had called Soul's manager, and he in turn had contacted Soul's personal physician and her publicist. All three were on their way.

A young doctor walked up to Jack and Izabel. 'I have good news,' he said, smiling. 'Your friend will be fine. Who administered CPR?'

'He did,' said Izabel and pointed to Jack.

'Well done; without that ...' The doctor shook her head.

'Any permanent damage?'

'Doesn't look like it.'

'Thank God,' said Izabel, tears streaming down her face. 'You should have seen him.'

The doctor nodded and walked away.

Izabel put her arms around Jack's neck. 'Thank you,' she whispered. 'You saved her life. I will never forget that.'

'Perhaps her good luck charm really works?'

'Her little cross? You know about that?' said Izabel, looking amazed. 'It did this time.'

'I hope it continues.'

Feeling drained, Jack left the hospital as soon as Soul's manager arrived, and went back to his hotel to pack. He was due to fly to Afghanistan the next day. There was nothing further he could do to help. Soul was in the best of care and appeared to be out of danger. On his way out, Jack told Izabel he would try to visit Soul before he left New York.

The next morning, Jack dropped into the hospital on his way to the airport. A security guard stationed in front of Soul's room asked him to wait. It was only after Soul's manager had given his okay that Jack was allowed to enter.

At first, Jack couldn't see the bed because of all the flowers in the room, which could easily have filled an entire Fifth Avenue florist. Izabel came over to Jack and kissed him on the cheek.

'So glad you could come. She's been asking about you all morning.'

'Are you sure she's in there somewhere?'

'I'm right here; come,' said Soul, her voice sounding strong and cheerful. Jack walked over to the bed and sat down on the edge.

'Not quite as pale as the last time I saw you,' he said, frowning.

Soul reached for his hand and for a long moment just held it without saying anything. 'They tell me I'm only alive because of you.'

'Doctors like to exaggerate.'

'Don't think so. Izabel was there, remember?'

'Right place; right time. That's all.'

Soul shook her head. 'There's more to it.' She held up the little cross. 'You were only there because of this.'

'True.'

'So, why don't you tell us why you are so interested in this little piece of jewellery?'

'There isn't all that much to tell. You would have heard most of it from your mother already. It all started with a deathbed revelation when my father died.'

'How fascinating,' said Izabel. 'In what way?'

Izabel sat down next to Jack on the bed and listened intently as he told them the story of his adoption and how he had only recently found out about it.

'This came as quite a shock, as you can imagine,' said Jack quietly. He then told them about his conversation with Gurrul, how he had found the old pawnbroker in Brisbane, and how the sale of the little Fabergé cross twenty-seven years ago had led him to Soul's parents, and to Soul.

'Amazing,' said Soul, running her fingertips along the little cross hanging around her neck. 'Are you suggesting this is the only link to your birth mother? The only clue about who she might have been?'

'Yes. Apparently it belonged to her, and she gave it away with her child.'

'How sad,' said Izabel.

'Both my adoptive parents are dead. The mission in Queensland where I was born was closed down a long time ago, and the cattle station where I grew up was sold off by the bank during a terrible drought.'

'So, this is all that's left?'

'Yes.'

'And you just wanted to have a look at it? Is that it? Is that why you made contact with me? Sentimentality?'

'There's a little more to it than that. The little cross is unique. The pawnbroker – an experienced jeweller – had no difficulty in identifying it as an original Fabergé piece made in Paris in the nineteen twenties. He suggested it may even have been a commission piece made to order, which was not unusual at the time. I was hoping to have a closer look at it, take a few photographs perhaps, to see if there are any identifying markings that could help me somehow trace, you know—'

'I understand,' said Soul. She took off the gold chain with the cross and handed it to Jack. 'Here, have a good look and by all means take photos. And while you do that, I'll tell you what *I* think.'

'All right.'

'I think it's all about destiny, and your extraordinary story proves it. All the pieces are falling into place.'

'In what way?'

'As you know, this used to belong to *my* mother, just as it appears to have belonged to yours. She gave it to me to protect me. Perhaps it was the same with you? And it did just that. You were waiting for me on the bridge and you saved my life. Coincidence? Hardly. It was meant to be. That's how I see it.'

'And that's how we shall leave it,' said Jack and handed the little cross back to Soul.

'I'll tell you something strange,' continued Soul, looking pensively at Jack. 'The only thing I remember about this whole episode is this: I remember seeing you standing on the bridge, waving. Then everything went blank. Nothing, until I woke up here in bed. But I do have a clear memory of one thing.'

'What's that?'

'A new song. Music, lyrics; the lot. I have already written it all down. It was like taking dictation. You want to know the title?'

'Tell me.'

'*Destiny*. The little cross brought us together and saved my life. If that isn't destiny, then …'

'I really have to go,' said Jack, changing the subject and standing up.

'You are going back to Afghanistan?' said Izabel.

'Yes. This afternoon. Back to the war. But before I go, there's one more thing …'

'Oh? What?' asked Soul.

'When someone saves someone's life, he owns part of it.'

'Says who?'

'Rules of destiny.'

'I see,' said Soul, smiling.

'And because he owns part of it, he's allowed to protect it and make a wish.'

'All right,' said Soul, wondering where Jack was going with this.

'I would like to protect the little part of your life I now own in a certain way.'

'How? Tell me.'

'Rehab.'

Soul bit her lip and stared at Jack. 'You know—' she began.

'Of course,' said Jack. 'I've seen it all before. But I may not be there the next time … Dicing with death can quickly land you in the Obituaries pages. I've seen that too.'

'Rehab? No lectures, no nagging, no—?'

'Just rehab. It's your choice.'

'He's right, darling,' said Izabel, reaching for Soul's hand.

'Come here, Jack,' said Soul and held up her arms.

Jack bent down and she kissed him tenderly on the mouth. 'Rehab it is.'

'You heard that, Izabel?' said Jack.

'I did.'

'Good.'

'And the wish?' asked Soul.

'That's a secret.'

'Ah. Take care of yourself, Jack,' said Soul, tears in her eyes, 'and stay in touch. We have a special bond, you and I.'

'Will do,' said Jack on his way to the door. 'And you take good care of our little cross – and that little part of your life that now belongs to me.

'I promise.'

HOSTAGE OF THE TALIBAN: 5 APRIL 2002

Jack had taken cover behind a rock and was furiously photographing the action erupting all around him. Excited and on an adrenaline high, he didn't fully appreciate the predicament they were in. The officer in charge had managed to call for reinforcements on his radio and was hoping his men could hold out until help arrived.

The US patrol had been mopping up pockets of Taliban resistance in a remote part of the Shai-Kot Valley, when it walked into an ambush. Surrounded, outnumbered and under heavy fire, the patrol had nowhere to go; it was only a matter of time before the six men would be overwhelmed by the heavily armed fighters attacking them from all sides.

The helicopter bringing in reinforcements came in low and was about to land when a rocket struck its tail, sending the chopper into a spin close to the ground. Moments later, it hit a rock close to Jack and burst into flames. The men jumping out of the burning cabin were instantly mowed down by machine-gun fire, their bullet-riddled bodies falling like bowling pins.

Oblivious to his own safety, Jack continued to take pictures. As he was only a few metres from the burning chopper, he could see the pilot desperately struggling to open the door from the inside of the badly damaged cabin. He appeared to be the only one still alive.

'Cover me, guys!' Jack heard someone shout from behind. Moments later, a soldier ran up to the chopper, opened the cabin door and was about to pull the injured pilot out into the open, when he was hit by several bullets from behind. Mortally wounded and still holding the pilot around the waist, he fell to the ground.

'*Get back!*' shouted a soldier next to Jack. 'She's about to blow!'

After that, Jack did something most others would have considered insane. He dropped his camera and ran towards the burning chopper. First, he pushed the dead soldier off the injured pilot. Then he dragged the young pilot away from the burning wreck just before it exploded in a ball of orange flames, knocking him to the ground.

The first thing Jack felt as he gained consciousness was a searing pain in his side. Then he opened his eyes. A man holding a candle was sitting next to him on the floor.

'You are awake; good,' he said in broken English. 'You lost a lot of blood.'

'Who are you? Where ...?'

'I am Mullah Shahzada. You are a prisoner of the Taliban.'

'The pilot?'

The man pointed to the other side of what looked like a dark cave with a low ceiling. 'Over there; alive.'

'The others?'

The man shrugged. 'A few got away. You are a journalist?' he said, holding up Jack's press card.

'I am.'

'Good. That's why you are still alive.'

'I don't understand.'

'You and the young American pilot over there have become famous overnight. The photos you took have made you a hero and you are therefore valuable. Very valuable. Negotiations are already in progress.'

'What negotiations?'

'A prisoner exchange.'

Shortly after the helicopter had exploded, a second one arrived and managed to drive back the Taliban fighters with rocket and machine-gun fire from above. Jack's discarded camera was found and the story – told by eyewitnesses who survived the ambush – of the heroic rescue of the injured pilot by the unarmed Australian journalist raced through the ranks like wildfire. Jack's subsequent capture by the Taliban added further interest and fascination to the story.

The army's publicity machine went into overdrive. Jack's photos were retrieved and the extraordinary pictures he had taken of the drama sent to his paper in New York for release. Within twenty-four hours, Jack's story was on every major news channel in the US and around the world. Suddenly, the war had a face, with a story of heroism and courage the people back home could relate to.

However, this put the High Command in Afghanistan under enormous pressure to facilitate the release and safe return of the captured pilot and the heroic-journalist who had saved his life. The stakes were high and the Taliban knew it. Negotiations began almost immediately. But the generals didn't like being held to ransom – literally. They decided on a different, more risky course of action that, if successful, would result in the happy ending everyone was hoping for. Without humiliation or loss of face.

Military intelligence on the ground pinpointed the likely location where the hostages were being held by the Taliban: a cave system in a remote part of the valley. It was decided that with the help of local scouts, a night raid by crack commandos was worth the risk. If it failed, the Taliban could be blamed for the loss of the hostages. If it succeeded, it would be a triumph.

The raid caught the Taliban unawares. Confident of a negotiated outcome, the fighters had let their guard down and were overpowered by the commandos storming the cave. However, in the desperate exchange of fire, Jack was shot in the leg and the young pilot was killed. So were all the Taliban fighters. Despite the mixed result, the publicity machine managed to put a favourable spin on the dramatic rescue, and pictures of a smiling Jack being carried on a stretcher to a waiting aircraft taking him to a military hospital in Germany were shown around the world. After that, the news cycle lost interest and moved on.

Jack stayed in hospital for two weeks until he was well enough to return to Australia for rehabilitation.

'That's him over there,' said the matron, looking at the tall, confident woman with interest. She pointed to a man sitting in a wheelchair under a tree. 'You can go and talk to him, if you like. He doesn't get many visitors.'

Ingrid Lloyd bit her lip, adjusted her hair and walked over to Jack, dozing in the sun. 'So, this is how a hero spends his afternoons,' she said. 'Napping on the job.'

Jack took off his straw hat and looked at Ingrid, surprised. 'Yesterday's heroes have little to do, I'm afraid. It's wonderful to see you. How did you find me?'

Ingrid bent down and kissed Jack on the cheek. *He's so thin*, she thought. 'My husband has excellent contacts. How are you?'

'Getting better. Please, take a seat.' Jack pointed to a wicker chair. 'The routine is relentless. Physio in the morning, followed by swimming, exercise bike and the wretched treadmill; day after day, watched over by imperious matrons who don't take no for an answer. You've just met one of them. But it's doing the job. I'm walking again. That's all that matters.'

'We saw it all on TV. Your adventure in Afghanistan. It was all over the news; amazing!'

Jack shrugged. 'One of those things you do, I suppose, when you're there and see it all happen. That's all.'

'Just as you did with Rachael?' said Ingrid, tears glistening in her eyes.

'Ah. She told you?'

'Yes, everything. My daughter is alive because of you. Words cannot express what I feel about that.'

'Has she told you about the little part of her life I own?'

'She has.'

'And is she looking after it?'

'She is, thanks to you. She cancelled her tour and is in rehab in California, making excellent progress. Working on her next album. I visited her last week.'

'Excellent. At least it hasn't been in vain then. Not like—'

'What?'

'The pilot,' said Jack, the sadness in his voice obvious. 'Life is so fragile and so uncertain. A young life snuffed out, just like that.'

'Do you want to know what the album is called?' asked Ingrid, trying to change an obviously painful subject.

'Tell me.'

'Destiny.'

'Ah.'

'And I believe you know why.'

Jack nodded. 'I know all about destiny. I've had a lot of time to think in here.'

'What are you going to do, when you—?'

'Get better?'

'Yes.'

'I need some stability in my life. My days as a war correspondent are over, that's for sure. I can't go back. I'm going to do something I've dreamt of doing since I was a kid.'

'What's that?'

'Writing.'

'What; *books?*'

'Yes. Deep down I'm a storyteller. I know that now. That's me. That's what I am; what makes me tick. That's my destiny. All I have to do is follow the breadcrumbs.'

'You are a lucky man, Jack.'

'In what way?'

'You appear to have found yourself. Not many do.'

'We'll soon see. I hope you're right.'

'Speaking of destiny,' said Ingrid, 'I have something for you.' She reached into her handbag, took out a little parcel wrapped in gold paper with a blue bow on top, and handed it to Jack. 'This is for you. From Rachael.'

'For me? How lovely. What is it?'

'Open it and see.'

When Jack untied the bow and peeled away the paper, he found a beautiful little wooden box inside. For a moment he held it up, a strange feeling washing over him. Then he opened it and gasped. '*It-it can't be,*' he stammered, a single tear running down his gaunt face as he gazed at the little gold cross with its precious stones sparkling in the morning sun.

Ingrid stood up and put her hand on Jack's shoulder. Her touch seemed to calm him. 'Before you get too excited,' she said, her voice quivering with emotion, 'it's not the original. Rachael would never part with that. It's a replica she had made for you.'

'It's beautiful,' whispered Jack. 'Would you please put it on for me?'

Ingrid took the little cross with the gold chain out of the box and fastened it around Jack's neck.

'Thank you,' said Jack, exploring the little cross with the tips of his fingers. 'I'll tell you something strange.'

'What?'

'Don't laugh.'

'I won't. Go on.'

'I no longer feel so alone.'

THE PORTRAIT: SYDNEY: MAY 2002

After several weeks of intense rehabilitation, Jack was finally well enough to be discharged. He was still walking with a limp and needed a walking stick to get around, but the freedom of living at home in Sydney without tedious regimentation and mind-numbing exercise routines, made up for it all.

Jack had always been interested in art, and one of his first outings was a visit to the Art Gallery of New South Wales to view the finalists of the coveted Archibald Prize, awarded annually for the best portrait. Jack had always preferred the popular People's Choice Award, which he considered a true reflection of popular art. Most of the time, the people's choice varied considerably from the judges' selections.

Taking his time, Jack made his way around the exhibition. He had to sit down regularly to ease the pain in his leg. As he sat down on one of the benches, he found himself facing the winner of the People's Choice Award; a large, black and white portrait of an elderly Aboriginal. For a while, he gazed at the man's striking face. Furrowed like the parched outback earth and with deep creases and wrinkles crisscrossing the forehead, they looked as if they could hold three days' rain.

Good God! It can't be, thought Jack as certain familiar features – especially the eyes, radiating intelligence and kindness – began to reach out to him, morphing slowly into recognition. Jack stood up and hobbled over to the painting for a closer look. *Incredible. It's him! Gurrul.*

The painting, by an unknown Aboriginal artist from Western Australia, was entitled *Gurrul dreaming of the past*. While the face itself was painted in black and white, the background depicted colourful rock art images of the Kimberley, especially Wandjina and the stick-like Bradshaw figures. In a strange way, the rock art reminded Jack of the murals he had just recently photographed in Bryn Evans's cell in Fremantle Prison.

As soon as he got home, Jack contacted one of the curators he knew well, to find out more about the winning painting and the artist. As it turned out, because the Aboriginal artist from the Kimberley and his subject were both unique and creating a lot of interest, one of the sponsors had offered to fly them both to Sydney for the presentation of the prize on the weekend. The curator made sure that Jack received an invitation.

Jack hadn't been in contact with Gurrul since the funeral. Because of his injuries and lengthy rehabilitation, Jack had lived like a hermit for weeks in almost total isolation and was only now beginning to slowly reconnect with friends and put his life back together.

As Jack got out of the taxi and hobbled up the stairs to the entrance of the Art Gallery, he still found it hard to believe that a portrait of Gurrul – his childhood friend and mentor – had won the People's Choice Award. Inside, the reception was already in full swing, with Sydney's social set rubbing shoulders with bohemian artists and haughty critics. Jack took a glass of champagne from a passing waiter and headed for one of the benches at the back of the hall. He was about to sit down and watch the colourful crowd when someone put a hand on his shoulder from behind.

'They told me you would be here, mate,' said a familiar voice. Startled, Jack turned around. Dressed in a pair of well-worn jeans, boots and a white shirt, Gurrul looked just like his portrait.

'We meet in strange places,' said Jack and embraced his friend. 'First a funeral, and now this—'

'As long as it's not your own, mate,' said Gurrul, laughing. 'I hear you came close.'

Jack waved dismissively. 'It was nothing.'

'Not what I heard.'

'You're famous.'

'Down here in the big smoke, perhaps. Back home, no-one cares.'

Gurrul broke off as the curator was making an announcement on the podium. 'Ladies and gentlemen, your attention please. It gives me great pleasure to introduce to you this year's winner of ...'

'Got to go, mate,' whispered Gurrul. 'Have to sing for my supper.'

'Dinner after the show?'

'You're on.'

After the speeches and presentation, Gurrul excused himself and met Jack at the exit, leaving the artist behind the podium to face the journalists by himself.

'They'll be mad at me for sneaking away like this for sure, but I don't care,' said Gurrul, getting into the taxi. 'I'd rather be with you, mate. This just isn't me.'

'You're a bloody philistine,' said Jack, laughing.

'A what?'

'Someone who doesn't give a stuff about an art prize.'

'That's about right. I'm starving.'

'A steakhouse by the harbour okay with you?'

'You bet. I could kill for a beer, mate.'

'So could I.'

The face that could hold three days' rain had a mouth that could devour two giant rib-eye steaks, which stunned the waiter and impressed the chef cooking at the open grill.

'That's better,' said Gurrul, downing his third beer. 'Great tucker.'

'How long are you staying?'

'Going back tomorrow. Can't wait. We are staying in a fancy joint somewhere near the airport.'

Feeling well-fed and relaxed after a few more beers, Jack decided to tell his friend what he had found out about his adoption so far. He sat back in his comfortable chair and pulled out the little gold cross from under his shirt.

'Here, have a look at this. Do you recognise it?'

Gurrul looked at the cross, his eyes wide with astonishment.

'Where on *earth* did you get this?' he asked, shaking his head.

'It's a long story.'

'We have all night, and the beer is cold.'

Jack told Gurrul about his breadcrumbs of destiny: the pawnbroker, Lloyd and Soul and how, and why, he had been given a replica of the cross.

'That's quite a story,' said Gurrul, shaking his head. 'Sounds like a movie, mate.'

'It does a bit. But I'm no closer—'

'To finding out who put the cross around your neck in the first place, and sent you out into the world – alone?'

Jack nodded. 'I made some enquiries through an auctioneer I know. Unfortunately, Fabergé records don't go back that far. The War ... But it was most likely a custom-made piece, made to order for a wealthy, probably Russian client.'

'A dead end, then?'

'Looks like it.'

'I did tell you to leave it alone, didn't I?'

'You did.'

'Any luck with the article?'

'As a matter of fact, yes. I found it—'

'And? More breadcrumbs?'

'You could say that.'

'And where did they take you?'

'To a card game in a pub in Broome and a priceless pearl called the Kimberley Queen that resulted in a fatal stabbing and a murder trial, and finally, a man called Bryn Evans who died tragically in Fremantle Prison in 1988.'

'You have been a busy boy.'

'Suppose so.'

'And?'

'If you are asking me if that man was my father, I honestly don't know. There's nothing to connect him to me apart from that one remark by Brother Francis you overheard at the mission all those years ago. And Brother Francis is long gone.'

'Another dead end, then?'

'Perhaps.' Jack shrugged. 'I tried to find out more about Bryn, but so far I've come up with nothing. Except for this.' Jack reached into his coat pocket, pulled out a few photographs and placed them on the table in front of him.

'What's this?'

'These are murals painted by Bryn on the walls of his cell in Fremantle jail. Because he was quite an accomplished artist they have been preserved as a curiosity, I suppose. The prison is now a World Heritage Site.'

'Show me.'

Jack pushed the photos across the table and for a while, Gurrul looked at them in silence.

'Bryn ran away after the stabbing and was arrested a couple of weeks later in a cave near Kalumburu, the Benedictine mission on the King Edward River in the Kimberley.'

'Interesting,' said Gurrul as he kept staring at the photos. 'I recognise all these places.'

'What do you mean?'

'These are all well-known locations in the Kimberley.' Gurrul held up one of the photos. 'Take this one, for instance,' he said. 'This is the wreck of a World War II DC3 that crash-landed near Kalumburu. It's still there. And this is Koolama Bay. And here, look, are the ruins of the Pago Mission near Faraway Bay. And this is a bend in the King Edward River some ten miles inland, with a cave covered in rock art.'

'What are you suggesting?' said Jack, leaning forward.

'These are memories ...'

'Memories of what?'

'A journey. It begins here at the top, at the mission – see? The first mural here is Kalumburu. No doubt about it. After that we go to the aircraft wreck, and then all the other places I mentioned.'

'Memories of a lonely, desperate prisoner occupying the same tiny cell for many years?'

'More than that. Recollections of a specific journey beginning at Kalumburu, and ending here.' Gurrul stabbed a finger at the last mural with the bloodstains, close to the cell door. 'I know this place.'

'You do?' said Jack.

'This is a spectacular rock art site in a cave on the King Edward River, not far from Kalumburu. Look, these are Wandjina images; some of the best preserved in the Kimberley. A whole row of them; a gallery. I actually did some work in there a few years ago, restoring the paintings.'

'Incredible!' Jack then told Gurrul about the bloodstains and how Bryn had died in his cell during the fire.

'So, this is the final mark he made on the cell wall with his fingertips before he died? With his own blood, right here on the last painting; see?'

'It would appear so.'

For a long moment, Gurrul peered at the photograph, lost in thought. 'I think he was trying to tell us something.'

'Come on ...'

'I'm serious. To me, these murals look like a map. My ancestors used to do a similar thing. They painted landmarks on rocks, guiding the tribe to precious waterholes and preserving the knowledge for generations to come by handing it down.'

Jack pointed to the mural with the bloodstains. 'Why this place? What was he trying to tell us?'

'Don't know, but we could try to find out.'

'How?'

'I could take you to it.'

'Are you serious?'

'Absolutely. I think a bit of time in the bush would do you good after all you've been through lately. Don't forget, I've known you since you were a nipper, Jack. *I know you.*'

'More breadcrumbs?'

'Could be. Why don't you come back to Wyndham with me tomorrow and we'll see?'

'Let's have another beer and I'll think about it.'

WANDJINA AND GWION: WYNDHAM: MAY 2002

Jack sat on the veranda of a small shack owned by Gurrul's cousin and watched the sun go down. Rocking back and forth in his chair with a beer in his hand, he was enjoying the splendid view across Wyndham Port and out towards the Cambridge Gulf, glistening in the distance. Established in the late eighteen-hundreds, Wyndham had serviced eager prospectors flocking to the Halls Creek gold rush.

The few carefree days in this remote Australian outpost with its colourful history had done wonders for Jack's recovery. Feeling relaxed and at home with his Aboriginal friends, he had gone fishing almost every day and taken the dogs for long walks along the foreshore. He was by now walking almost without a limp, and didn't need the walking stick.

'I reckon a couple more days and you'll be ready to take the trip up the river with me,' said Gurrul, watching Jack.

'Can't wait.' Jack lifted his glass and looked at his friend. 'Thanks for bringing me here, mate. Exactly what I needed. Somehow, everything looks a lot clearer from up here.'

Gurrul nodded. 'This place is not only ancient, it's timeless. That's why I love living in the Kimberley. It's a spiritual place. Wait till you see the rock art ...'

'So, what do you think about the murals now?' asked Jack, pointing to the photographs on the table in front of him.

'Well, I look at it this way: the guy is serving a life sentence for murder and is locked up in this tiny cell, which has become his world. All he has left to connect him to the outside, to freedom, are his memories. So, he decides to paint the walls of his cell – his world – capturing the most precious memories he has and wants to be reminded of.'

'Makes sense.'

'But I don't believe these murals were painted entirely at random.'

'What do you mean?'

'These are all iconic places up here in the Kimberley, and they are all reasonably close to Kalumburu, the Benedictine mission. Look here: Koolama Bay, Faraway Bay, then the Pago ruins of the old mission and so on. You said the guy was a pearler from Broome. He obviously knew this remote coast well and had access by boat – which is often the only way to reach these places.'

'What's your point?'

'Look at the last three murals. First, a few men playing cards – obviously a winning poker hand – see the Royal Flush? And a huge pearl. The Kimberley Queen? The winnings? Then the next one here is Kalumburu; you can clearly make out the mission buildings. But the most interesting painting is the last one here at the bottom, near the door to the cell.'

'The one with the bloodstains?' said Jack.

'Yes. It depicts a spectacular rock art site; a cave-like overhang on the King Georges River near Kalumburu that I know well. It's surprisingly accurate, bearing in mind it was painted from memory. You said Bryn was arrested in a cave near the mission?'

'He was.'

'And the pearl was never found?'

'No. He didn't have it on him.'

'Hardly surprising, is it?'

'What are you suggesting?'

'Tell me, what would you do? You are on the run with a priceless pearl in your possession. Trackers are closing in and you know you will soon be found and arrested. Time's running out,' said Gurrul, becoming excited.

'I would hide the precious pearl.'

'Exactly. In a safe, but identifiable place – just in case.'

'And then make a record of it on the wall of my prison cell? Come on ...'

'Why not? A small act of defiance of a desperate, lonely man with a sense of humour and nowhere to go. Can you see the irony?'

'Sure can,' said Jack thoughtfully, looking out to sea. 'It's a long shot for sure, but—'

'Worth considering don't you think, mate? To me, the clincher is this: the guy is injured and dying in his cell. What's the last thing he does? He makes a mark on this painting here with his fingertips, using his own blood.'

'X marks the spot? The hiding place, you reckon?'

'Let's find out.'

'Tomorrow?'

'If you think you're up to it,' said Gurrul, laughing.

'Sure am, mate. Let's have another beer.'

Jack and Gurrul left for Kalumburu early the next morning. Gurrul explained to Jack that the Kimberley was roughly the size of Germany – isolated, remote, rugged and dangerous, it wasn't a place to venture without a guide. Because they had to carry everything, progress was slow in the rugged terrain. The stunning rock formations along the river were dotted with Aboriginal burial sites – skulls and bones on rock shelves exposed to the elements – whispering of generations past. Several rock faces along the way were covered in rock art; Wandjinas as well as the much older Bradshaws.

'Dating rock art is very difficult,' said Gurrul. 'Due to contamination, Uranium Series dating was unsuccessful.'

'What about carbon dating?'

'That also failed because the paintings don't contain organic material,' Gurrul explained, sitting down on a rock. 'Here,' he said, pulling a tatty-looking pamphlet out of his backpack and handing it to Jack. 'It's all in there.'

Jack thumbed through the pages and read:

The most accurate dating came about entirely by accident: an ancient, fossilised wasp nest built on top of one of the rock paintings a long time ago. Using an amazing technique called optical-stimulated luminescence, scientists were able to accurately date the wasp nest. It had been built on top of the painting by industrious mud wasps 16,000 years ago, thereby establishing a benchmark minimum age of the painting …

'Fascinating,' said Jack, handing the pamphlet back to Gurrul.

'Sure is, mate.'

By midmorning the heat was almost unbearable. Jack took off his backpack and sat down in the shade under a rock overhang overlooking a bend in the river below.

'I need a drink,' he said, and reached for his water bottle. 'How much further?'

'Three hours, I'd say,' said Gurrul, sitting down beside him. 'Bloody hot today.'

'Bradshaws?' said Jack, pointing to some paintings on the rock behind him.

Gurrul nodded. 'We call them Gwion.' He rummaged in his backpack and retrieved the old pamphlet again. 'Have a read while we take a break – it's interesting,' he said.

Jack found the page he was looking for and read aloud: 'Explorer, and future South Australian governor, Sir George Grey mentioned rock art in the Kimberley as early as 1838. The rock art he recorded was the Wandjina art form, depicting mythological cloud and rain spirits. Experts suggest that this particular art form reaches back four thousand years or more.

'However, while searching for suitable grazing land in a remote part of the Kimberley in 1891, pastoralist Joseph Bradshaw discovered something unusual on a rugged sandstone escarpment: a striking type of rock art that was quite different from the Wandjina style he had encountered before.'

'Yep, and the local Aboriginals referred to this ancient art as Gwion Gwion,' said Gurrul. 'We have a treasure-trove of Gwions up here,' he continued, pointing to the decorated rock wall behind him. 'There are many types of Gwions; some quite small like these, while others are up to three metres high. Take the Ngunuru Gwion – tall, long bodies with ceremonial headdresses and wearing armbands, skirts and tassels – they are quite distinctive, and so are the Yowana Gwions and the

Dynamic Gwions, running and hunting with spears. Some archaeologists reckon they could be more than fifty thousand years old. Very different from the Wandjina.'

'You certainly seem to know a lot about this stuff.'

'You learn a lot from the elders when you live up here – and listen.'

It took Jack and Gurrul another five hours to reach their destination. Jack was limping badly by then and could hardly walk. His feet were swollen, and he had blisters on his heels. But all this was forgotten when they approached the spectacular Wandjina site – a large, cave-like rock overhang above a waterfall, almost hidden behind a thick curtain of vegetation.

Jack took off his backpack and his boots, and looked up in wonder at the striking paintings stretching for several metres along a smooth rock wall. 'Wow! I've never seen anything like this before,' he said.

'Thought you'd be impressed. These are some of the best preserved Wandjinas in the Kimberley. It's very unusual to find so many next to each other in a row, and so big. That's why I recognised them straight away when you showed me the photo of the mural.'

'So, Wandjinas are mythological beings?' said Jack as he glimpsed up at the six stunning creatures, looking like aliens from a different, mysterious world. The striking colours of black, red and yellow on a white background, accentuated the large upper bodies and heads with eyes and nose, but no mouth. According to legend, these creatures were so powerful they didn't require speech, and it was said that if they did have mouths, the rain would never stop. And perhaps most striking of all were the arced lines around the heads, like haloes, representing lighting coming out of helmets, reminiscent of astronauts.

'They are,' replied Gurrul. 'And they have to be treated with respect. We repaint the images in December or January to ensure the Wandjina stay with us, and secure the arrival of the monsoon rains.'

'Incredible.'

'But it's very unusual to find six of them painted in a row like this. This must have been a very important ceremonial site,' continued Gurrul. 'A place of ancient rituals and secrets.'

'Well, do you reckon Bryn has hidden the Kimberley Queen somewhere in here? Among mythological guardians?'

Jack reached into his backpack, pulled out a photograph and held it up. 'An excellent likeness,' he said.

'The bloody finger marks are somewhere around here,' said Gurrul, pointing to the last two Wandjinas in the row above.

Jack shook his head. 'Needle in a haystack, wouldn't you say? Even if you're right, it could be anywhere.'

'Who said it was going to be easy? Let's have something to eat first, then we search the place.'

'You're on!'

Jack and Gurrul searched every corner of the site until the shadows lengthened and the sun went down. Methodically, they explored every crack in the decorated rock face and ran their fingers down grooves and clefts until their fingertips bled and their necks hurt from looking up.

Then Gurrul lit a fire, boiled some water in the billy and made tea. 'We'll have another look in the morning,' he said, trying to sound cheerful.

'I'm buggered,' said Jack, sipping his tea and looking up at the stars blazing above. 'But I'm glad you brought me here, even if this turns out to be a wild goose chase – as I strongly suspect it will,' he added, laughing.

'I knew the trip would do you good. After Afghanistan, and the funeral ... You're turning over a new page in your life. There's no better place to do that than right here. It puts the world, and us, into perspective.' Gurrul reached for his tobacco pouch and rolled himself a smoke. 'My dad used to take me out into the bush when I was a youngster and teach me stuff about the past. I remember sitting with him under the stars just like this, and listening to Dreamtime stories ... And now here we are, you and me.'

Jack stretched out on top of his swag and looked down to the river, glistening in the soft moonlight below. It was a magical moment, conjuring up memories of his own childhood and his father whom he had recently buried. As his aching body relaxed and his eyelids became heavier, Jack drifted towards much-needed sleep, despite unsettling questions about Bryn Evans and his tragic life keeping him awake. Finally, overcome by fatigue, he fell into a restless slumber.

Jack woke with a start, and for a while listened to the silence, trying to orientate himself. Then he opened his eyes and looked around. Bathed in bright moonlight, the rocks along the banks of the river below looked like ruins of an ancient fortress, guarding the river and its secrets. Gurrul was asleep on top of his swag on a rock ledge nearby, his regular, deep breathing the only sound.

Rubbing his aching neck, Jack looked up at the Wandjinas watching him, he felt, from above. Fingers of moonlight reached through the vegetation into the large cave, illuminating their faces with shafts of ghostly light, almost bringing them to life as they gazed into eternity. As Jack looked along the row of mysterious faces, his eyes came to rest on the second last one. Its face was white, the large eyes and long nose outlined in ochre, and there was no mouth. But Jack noticed that one eye was strikingly different. Reflecting the moonlight, it seemed to be alive, staring directly down at him.

How weird, thought Jack and sat up. The Wandjina eye appeared to follow him. Instead of banishing the illusion, the new angle seemed to make the eye stand out even more, making it sparkle and appear brighter still.

Good God; could it be? thought Jack as he remembered the bloodstain on the mural in Bryn Evans's prison cell. Jack stood up and walked into the cave for a closer look. But as he approached the painting, the face slipped back into darkness and the eye disappeared.

Jack couldn't reach the face of the large Wandjina looming above him, even by standing on the tips of his toes. It was too high up. Instead, he climbed up onto a narrow ledge above the head, to reach down from above. Jack went down on his knees and, his hand shaking, began to explore the face with the tips of his fingers.

As expected, the left eye was smooth, painted rock. Feeling his way, Jack reached the right eye. *I don't believe it!* he thought as his fingertips touched something set into the rock, like an eye set into its socket. The object could be moved about easily and Jack removed it slowly with shaking fingers. *Don't drop it, for Christ's sake!* he told himself, his heart beating like a drum.

Clutching the smooth, round heavy object the size of a sparrow's egg in his closed fist, Jack climbed carefully down from the ledge, went outside, and stepped into the moonlight. Taking a deep breath he opened his fist, and gasped. He was looking at the legendary Kimberley Queen, the largest pearl ever found in Australian waters.

THE PEARL BARON: MAY 2002

Benedict Morgan – an early riser – sat by the open window of his Broome office, overlooking the small port. It was just after sunrise and one of the diving vessels was preparing to leave port, headed for the company's pearl farm in Cygnet Bay. BM PEARLS, a multimillion dollar business, was one of the world's leading producers of cultured pearls. Famous for their size and lustre, the coveted pearls were in great demand by those rich enough to be able to afford them.

Despite being well into his eighties and confined to a wheelchair, Benedict Morgan still had a firm grip on the family company's rudder, and had steered the business through many a storm since he had taken over the helm from his father sixty years ago.

Morgan put down his binoculars and called Imogen Turnbull, the manager of the company's opulent Sydney showroom in Martin Place, where several necklaces had a price tag of more than a million dollars and some unique individual pearls cost more than a hundred thousand.

'You saw the article in today's *Australian*, I take it?' asked Morgan, staring at the article on his open iPad. He didn't believe in small talk or polite chit-chat.

'Of course. And so did many in the business, especially our competitors. I already had a few calls.'

'What do you think? Could it be the Kimberley Queen?'

'The auctioneers seem to think so. They claim to have done extensive checking. They are very confident.'

'What about the guy—?'

'Jack Rogan, the one who claims to have found it?'

'Yes. What's known about him?'

'He's a journalist with quite a reputation.'

'What kind of reputation?'

'He's a war correspondent and a hero; a colourful character.'

'Where's he now?'

'In Sydney, I believe. Why?'

'Good. Now listen carefully, this is what I want you to do …'

Jack looked at the elegant young woman sitting in the comfortable leather seat next to him as the small private jet taxied slowly along the runway, preparing for take-off. Used mainly to fly prospective buyers to Broome to entertain them in the Kimberley and show them the company's exotic pearling operation in Cygnet Bay, the *Black Pearl* – BM PEARLS' company jet – was the epitome of luxury and designed to impress.

'I love the take-off,' said Imogen, tightening her seatbelt. 'The sheer power of this thing. We can have some champagne as soon as we are in the air. As a little thank you …' Used to dealing with men and well aware of the effect she had on them, Imogen put her hand on Jack's arm and gave him her best smile.

'A thank you for what?'

'Not everyone is prepared to drop everything after a brief telephone conversation out of the blue, come to the airport and fly to Broome at an hour's notice to meet a stranger.'

'Suppose not. But I'm used to stuff like this. In my line of business, the unusual is the norm. Most of the time you have to act on the spur of the moment, make snap decisions and take risks.'

He and Morgan will get on well, *thought Imogen, smiling.*

'But it's usually noisy helicopter gunships I hitch a ride in, not posh private jets like this one,' continued Jack. 'With sweaty soldiers going into battle, not cultured women wearing Chanel number 5.'

'How on earth did you know?'

'Good nose. And besides, I love Chanel 5,' said Jack, touching his nose and laughing. 'Certain girlfriends are hard to forget,' he added, lowering his voice.

'What an exciting life you lead, Mr Rogan,' said Imogen, enjoying the company of the intriguing man next to her. She had to admit, the morning had gone far better than expected. Contacts at the paper had given her Jack's phone number. Her conversation with Jack early that morning had been brief and to the point. Just as her boss would have liked. Once she had explained who she was, Imogen extended an invitation on behalf of Benedict Morgan, the famous pearl baron, to fly to Broome later that day for a meeting to discuss the Kimberley Queen.

To her surprise, instead of meeting annoyed resistance, or at least a raft of prickly questions, Jack had readily agreed and met her at the airport two hours later. What Imogen couldn't have known, of course, was the real reason behind Jack's unexpected cooperation. As soon as he heard who wanted to meet him and why, Jack couldn't believe his luck and looked at the unexpected invitation as another one of his 'breadcrumbs of destiny'.

Perched on a cliff above Cable Beach and surrounded by manicured tropical gardens, the Morgan family residence – a large Queenslander – had uninterrupted views of the Indian Ocean and the beach below. Morgan lived in the house alone but for his housekeeper, a Chinese cook, and an elderly Aboriginal driver.

Morgan was sitting on the veranda watching the spectacular sunset when his housekeeper announced the arrival of his guests.

'Thank you for humouring an old man, Mr Rogan,' said Morgan, extending his hand, 'I really appreciate you coming here, and at such short notice.' Morgan paused, sizing up his visitor. 'Imogen must have been very persuasive,' he added, a sparkle in his eyes.

'She didn't have to be,' replied Jack casually. 'I was a willing participant.'

'He was,' said Imogen.

'How so?'

'Because I wanted to meet you; perhaps more than you wanted to meet me.'

Morgan looked at Jack, bemused. 'You wanted to meet me because—?'

'I would like to talk to you about a poker game, a priceless pearl and a fatal stabbing.'

'What's your interest in all this?' interrupted Morgan, frowning.

'It's a long story; a painful one.'

'For you or for me?'

'For both of us.'

'I'm intrigued. Care to explain?'

'Sure.'

During the next hour, Jack told Morgan that he was on a quest; a quest to discover his true identity. He explained how he had recently found out about his adoption just before his father died, and how his 'breadcrumbs of destiny' had led him to the Kimberley Queen on the banks of the King George River a few days ago.

As the sun approached the horizon, it lit up the sky in spectacular shades of orange and red so bright that it hurt the eyes. For a while, the two men sat in silence and watched the sun sink into the sea as the day died, and night approached in sombre shades of mauve, like a celestial blanket putting the waves to sleep.

'That's quite a story, Mr Rogan,' said Morgan, breaking the silence.

'It is, but for me there is no ending; not yet. Not until I find out who—'

'Your parents are? And you think I can help you?'

'Perhaps. Perhaps we can help each other.'

'How?'

'As you obviously know, I am about to send the Kimberley Queen to London for auction. You can imagine, the interest has already been considerable. And the story I just told you will form part of the pearl's unique provenance, adding some romance and excitement to the sale. However, this could open old wounds …'

This guy's good, thought Morgan, recognising in Jack a skilled negotiator and clever tactician. 'What's your point?' he asked.

Jack turned to Imogen sitting quietly behind them, listening intently. 'Miss Turnbull told me you are interested in acquiring the Kimberley Queen. That is the reason you brought me here – right?'

Morgan nodded.

'I can well understand why. The legendary pearl has been in your family since it was discovered in 1905, and its loss – especially in such tragic circumstances was—'

'Painful and regrettable; correct,' interrupted Morgan with sadness in his voice.

'Perhaps we can make a deal?'

'What kind of deal?'

Leaning back in his chair, Jack reached into his pocket, pulled out a small leather pouch and placed it on the table in front of Morgan. 'Please open it,' he said.

'Imogen, would you?' said Morgan, observing Jack carefully.

Imogen walked over to the table, picked up the pouch, looked inside – and gasped. Taking a deep breath, she reached inside and carefully pulled out a large pearl, and handed it to her boss. Morgan held it up to the light, his hand shaking, and stared at it for a while as he remembered his only son, and the part the exquisite pearl had played in his tragic death.

'The traveller returns; amazing,' whispered Morgan, shaking his head and placing the pearl on top of the pouch. 'After all these years ... So, what's on your mind, Mr Rogan?'

'Would you agree that this is the Kimberley Queen?'

'It is; no doubt about it.'

'I believe the pearl belongs here, with you,' said Jack. 'It shouldn't leave Australia.'

'I agree, but it now belongs to *you*,' said Morgan, once again watching Jack carefully.

'Here's the deal: I'll sell you the Kimberley Queen before auction, in exchange for—'

'What?' interrupted Morgan, a little annoyed. He wasn't used to having terms dictated to him.

'Information.'

'What kind of information?'

'Why two close friends fell out and became such bitter enemies, and what really happened in China Lane on that fateful night.'

'You want to know about the woman, don't you?'

'Yes.'

'Because she could be—'

'My mother.'

'I see. And the price?'

'I'll leave that up to you. I'm sure you'll give me a fair price, and I don't believe there is anyone better qualified to determine what that price should be than you. That's good enough for me.'

'Fair enough. Why don't we have some dinner first and discuss this later?' said Morgan, turning his wheelchair around. 'I have a wonderful cook, and you and Imogen have had a long day.'

'Sounds great.'

'I hope you like seafood. Patrick has been preparing my meals for over thirty years. He makes some of the best curries in the Kimberley.'

'I can't wait.'

Jack and Imogen flew back to Sydney early the next morning. As the plane reached cruising altitude and levelled out, Imogen turned to Jack sitting next to her. 'That was quite something last night,' she said, putting her hand on Jack's.

'It was the right way.'

'You brought some sunshine into a lonely old man's life.'

'The Kimberley Queen?'

'It means a lot to him.'

'I could see that.'

'What about you? Did you find what you were looking for?'

'Another piece in the puzzle, certainly, but—'

'Still a long way to go?'

'Yes. But I do feel I'm a little closer than I was before. You heard—'

'That Andy was infatuated with a beautiful French girl with a Russian name?'

'Mr Morgan unfortunately couldn't remember it.'

'She fell in love with Bryn Evans, his son's best friend, and ran away with him.'

'But what could be helpful here is this,' said Jack. 'Apparently, she was a freelance photographer working on an assignment for *National Geographic* at the time and was doing a piece on the pearl divers of the Kimberley. If such a piece was published, then ...'

'You should be able to trace it.'

'Exactly.'

'And China Lane?'

Jack shook his head and looked down at the arid, red Australian landscape gliding past below. 'I don't think anyone will ever know what really happened there. Andy was stabbed to death, and Bryn was convicted of his murder and died in jail. These are the sad facts. Nothing can change that.'

'What are you going to do with the money?' asked Imogen, changing the subject. 'It's a small fortune.'

'I'm going to buy a house. A home at last. I need an anchor in my life.'

'A new beginning?'

'I hope so.'

'I wish you well, Jack,' said Imogen. She leaned across and kissed Jack tenderly on the cheek. 'Keep following your breadcrumbs of destiny. I hope you find what you are looking for.'

'So do I. Any champagne left?'

'Sure.'

'Then, let's drink to that.'

THE BALLERINA IN THE NURSING HOME: 2012

The sale of the Kimberley Queen changed Jack's life. He bought a terrace house in Sydney, stopped being a war correspondent, drank a little less and began to write. Not just articles, but in earnest. Short stories at first, but this soon developed into a passion that was to stay with him for the rest of his life. A strong believer in destiny, Jack knew that the best stories would always find *him;* all he had to do was follow the breadcrumbs and his instincts.

After a passionate affair, Imogen moved in with Jack. Unfortunately, the relationship was stormy and didn't last; two years later, they drifted apart.

There was one more encouraging twist in Jack's search for his biological parents before the search reached a frustrating dead end. Following the lead provided by Benedict Morgan, Jack managed to track down an article in the December 1968 issue of *National Geographic* entitled *The Pearl Divers of the Kimberley.* When he discovered that the article featured a collection of stunning photographs by a freelance photographer from Paris with a Russian-sounding name, Jack was sure he was on the right track at last.

Several of the photographs featured iconic places in the Kimberley that he recognised. However, what was even more telling was the fact that some of these places were depicted in the murals of Bryn Evans's prison cell, providing a compelling link between Bryn and the photographer. Jack thought his breadcrumbs of destiny were finally reaching their destination.

Unfortunately, he soon realised this was not to be, when it transpired that the photographer had used a *nom de plume* for her articles – Natasha Rostova. It appeared that all his efforts to identify and track her down had failed.

This was where the matter rested, until an unexpected encounter ten years later with a fascinating old lady in an exclusive nursing home in France changed everything. By then, Jack had written several highly successful books, one of which – *Dental Gold and other Horrors* – propelled him into the spotlight and onto the front cover of *Time* magazine as a celebrated author with a mission.

It had all begun with another adventure: the dramatic rescue of Countess Kuragin's daughter, Anna, who had been abducted in Outback Australia in 2005 and disappeared, presumed dead. The circumstances of her dramatic rescue in the remote Kimberley wilderness in Western Australia in 2010 made headlines around the world, adding another chapter to Jack's growing fame and international standing.

Eternally grateful for the return of her lost daughter and a grandson she didn't know she had, Countess Kuragin took Jack into her heart and into her home, and a close friendship was forged. Jack, who was unattached and living by himself at the time, effectively became a member of the Kuragin family and spent several months a year at the Kuragin Chateau just outside Paris, writing. It was during this period that an unexpected breakthrough came that was to change Jack's life – once again, in a most unexpected way.

Jack was working on his next book, following the trail of a notorious Nazi who had spent time in the famous Ritz in Paris during the war with Reichsmarschall Göring, Hitler's second-in-command.

Frustrated by the lack of records and eyewitness accounts, Jack was feeling quite low and dejected.

'Don't look so glum; it's not like you, Jack,' said the countess and handed him a cup of tea in the conservatory overlooking the garden, which was Jack's favourite writing spot. 'You've been moping around for days …'

Jack pushed his keyboard aside and looked at the countess. 'You don't know what it's like banging your head against a brick wall, just when things become really interesting …'

'Then let me help you pull down the wall.'

'How exactly?'

The countess reached for Jack's hand. 'Come with me; we are going for a little drive.'

'Oh? A picnic perhaps to cheer me up?' said Jack, a sparkle in his eyes. 'To rejuvenate the creative spirit, like last time?'

'No. I want you to meet someone who may help you demolish that annoying wall that's giving you writer's block.'

'Who?'

'A Russian ballerina.'

'How exciting!'

'Anastasiya Petrova was already famous in her early teens,' said the countess as they drove through the ornate wrought-iron gates. The exclusive retirement home, a converted chateau, was popular with well-heeled aristocrats and celebrities. 'She was one of the baby ballerinas of the Ballet Russe de Monte Carlo and later became a film star. She was also one of my mother's closest friends.'

'I can't wait.'

'You won't be disappointed.'

'And we are going to meet her because …?'

'She lived at the Ritz during the war.'

'Wow!'

A nurse in a crisp uniform who seemed to know the countess well, welcomed them in the entry foyer and showed them to Madame Petrova's room on the ground floor. 'She's expecting you,' said the nurse, opening the door to a large room overlooking the manicured grounds.

Madame Petrova sat in a chair facing the open window. Elegantly dressed in a tight-fitting black dress and wearing a priceless string of baroque pearls and a pair of beautiful earrings that whispered Tiffany, she certainly had presence – even in her nineties. "Elegance and style are timeless" was her motto, and she lived by it. Her snow-white hair was pulled back and tied in a neat bun, exposing a long, swanlike neck. Impeccable make-up accentuated her prominent cheekbones and made her almond-shaped, slightly slanted eyes look large, giving her an exotic, almost feline look.

'How wonderful of you to come, my dear,' said Madame Petrova in French, struggling to stand up with the aid of a walking stick she hated. 'I saw you arrive.'

The countess walked over to her friend and kissed her on both cheeks. 'I've brought someone who wants to meet you,' she said in English.

'A young man; how exciting,' said Madame Petrova, switching to perfect English. 'Please come a little closer so I can see you.' She refused to wear glasses 'in public'.

'He's a writer,' said the countess, lowering her voice. She knew this would excite her friend even more. Madame Petrova had a soft spot for writers.

'So, you want to know about the Ritz during the war,' said Madame Petrova after the maid had served petits fours and tea. 'It was without doubt the most exciting time of my life; but dangerous,' Madame Petrova paused, and let her eyes roam over the photographs on the grand piano next to her.

'What made it so dangerous and exciting?' asked Jack.

'The people. Especially the Germans. Here, have a look.' Madame Petrova pointed to the photographs on the piano, her fingers shaking. Jack noticed her parchment-like skin was almost translucent.

'That's Reichsmarschall Göring with von Stulpnagel, the military commander of occupied Paris. Göring was crazy, but everyone was dancing around him like moths drawn to a flame. And here, that's Canaris, head of the Abwehr, the German intelligence offices in Paris. He was a double agent.'

Madame Petrova pointed to another sepia photograph. 'The man next to him is von Choltitz, a general. He was in charge during the last days of the German occupation. He defied Hitler and refused to burn Paris. As you can see, all these photographs were taken at the Ritz. And look, over here; that's me standing next to Charles Ritz, Coco Chanel and Marlene Dietrich. You know what Charles used to say?' Jack shook his head. 'Luxury stains everyone it touches. It certainly did.'

'And then there were the writers. You would be interested in that,' continued Madame Petrova, becoming animated. 'That's Jean-Paul Sartre and Simone de Beauvoir; Hemingway's drinking buddies. My God, we had some wild times together.' Exhausted by the memories of her youth, Madame Petrova slumped back into her chair. As she reached for the armrest, the little plate in her lap fell to the floor, sending a puff of icing sugar dancing across the carpet.

As Jack bent down to pick it up, Madame Petrova saw the little cross dangling around his neck. Her eyes widened with astonishment as she stared at it. 'Wh-where did you get this?' she stammered, and pointed to the cross. 'May I have a look?'

'Of course.' Jack took off the chain and handed the cross to Madame Petrova.

'Mon Dieu!' she exclaimed. 'It can't be.'

Noticing the distress on her friend's face, the countess stood up, walked over to the old lady and put her hand on her bony shoulder to calm her. 'What is it, my dear?' she asked.

Madame Petrova pointed to a little ivory box on the piano. 'Please, give it to me.'

The countess reached for the little box on the piano behind her and handed it to her friend. Madame Petrova opened it, her fingers shaking. Then she reached inside, lifted out a little jewel-encrusted gold cross, and placed it carefully on the table next to Jack's. The two crosses were identical.

Barely able to control his excitement, Jack began to question Madame Petrova about her cross.

'Please, not so fast,' interrupted the old lady, holding up a shaking hand. 'If you live life in the rear-view mirror like I do, things become a little blurred.'

Obviously exhausted, Madame Petrova sank back into her chair again, looking quite frail. The sparkle ignited by her memories had gone out. All that remained was an emotional little old lady, struggling with the present. 'The nurse will come any moment. It's time for my pills and my nap,' she said. 'The pills keep my body alive, but do little for my spirit.'

'We should go,' said the countess to Jack, standing quickly.

'Perhaps tomorrow,' said Madame Petrova. 'Yes, please come back tomorrow. We can visit my memory trees, and I'll tell you all about the cross ...'

For a long moment, Madame Petrova stared at the two crosses on the table in front of her. Then she lifted her eyes and looked pleadingly at Jack. It was a look Jack would never forget. 'Could you please leave your cross with me overnight?' she whispered. 'It will help me dream of the past, and prepare me for tomorrow.'

'Certainly, Madame,' said Jack, deeply moved. Then he took a bow, and followed the countess to the door.

Madame Petrova's Memory Trees: 2012

Jack and the countess returned to the nursing home the next morning.

'What did you make of yesterday?' asked Jack as they drove through the gates.

'Her body's frail, but her mind is as sharp as ever.'

'I barely slept a wink last night. I had this feeling—'

'What kind of feeling?'

'Destiny, closing in.'

The countess shook her head. 'You and destiny ...'

'I can't help it.'

'We'll know soon enough. I rang the nurse earlier. She said Madame Petrova was ready and waiting.'

'Ready for what, I wonder?'

'To visit her memory trees, of course. Don't you remember?'

Jack shook his head. 'This is really weird. Do you know what that's all about?'

'I do.'

'Are you going to tell me?'

'No. I think it's better if you find out for yourself. Look, we're almost there,' said the countess.

'More breadcrumbs?'

'Could be.'

'You're teasing me.'

'Perhaps just a little.'

Madame Petrova was waiting for them in her room, only this time she was sitting in a wheelchair. Impeccably dressed, just like the day before, she looked relaxed and composed.

'I don't like this contraption,' she said, pointing to the wheelchair, 'but as we are going outside, it's a necessity I'm sad to say.' Madame Petrova turned to Jack. 'But before we go, I would like to ask you something.'

'Please, go ahead,' said Jack.

Madame Petrova held up Jack's little cross. 'Please tell me how you came by this. Only two were ever made, right here in Paris. My father designed them and Alexander Fabergé made them, personally. They were close friends, you see. My father gave them to my sister and me as special Easter presents in 1930. Fabergé crosses instead of Fabergé eggs ...'

The countess shot Jack a meaningful look.

Jack waited until the maid had served tea and left the room. Then he told the story of the little cross, and explained its significance and what it meant to him, and why. Madame Petrova listened without interrupting, and for a while even closed her eyes. Jack thought she had fallen asleep, but when she began to ask pointed questions, he realised she had been listening to every word.

'Are you telling me this cross here is the only link to your birth mother?'

'That's right.'

'And you have been trying to find out who she was ever since your father told you about your adoption just before he died in 2002?'

'Yes, unfortunately I've had little success. Even the name in that article in the *National Geographic* I mentioned turned out to be a dead end.'

Madame Petrova began to chuckle. 'Natasha Rostova, a character out of Tolstoy's *War and Peace*. How typical. She always had a wonderful sense of humour—'

'Who?' asked the countess.

Madame Petrova held up her hand. 'Later, my dear,' she said. 'And you were born on the Coberg Mission in Queensland, Australia, Mr Rogan? In 1968?'

'That's right,' said Jack, startled by Madame Petrova's accurate recollection of what he had told her earlier.

'That too, fits,' said Madame Petrova, a knowing smile creasing the corners of her mouth. 'And Sister Elizabeth knew your mother well, you say?'

'It would appear so.'

'Astonishing. And you had this cross here around your neck when you were presented to your adoptive parents as a baby?'

Jack nodded. 'That's what I was told.'

'This is God's work,' said Madame Petrova, becoming emotional. She reached for Jack's hand and held it tight. 'A gift to an old woman at the end of her days.'

'What kind of gift?' asked Jack, looking puzzled.

'You.'

'What do you mean?' asked the countess, frowning.

'Let's go outside to visit my memory trees, and I'll tell you.'

Following Madame Petrova's directions, Jack pushed the wheelchair along a shady path leading to a pond with waterlilies. 'This magnificent estate used to belong to a duchess; a dear friend of mine,' said Madame Petrova. 'Before she turned it into a nursing home for artists and friends. This is her legacy. An extraordinary idea, don't you think? We spent many a summer here together. She was a great patron of the arts.'

'She certainly was that,' said the countess. 'My mother spent her last few years here, in the room right next to yours.'

'Ah yes. She was a wonderful friend. That's her tree right there. We planted it together, remember?'

The countess nodded.

'But I'm the last one,' continued Madame Petrova. 'I don't really know any of the others staying here now. They are all so young. It has become a very lonely life – old age ... All I have left are my memories and my trees, over there.' Madame Petrova pointed to a grove of oak trees by the pond. 'Let's go over there and I will introduce you.'

The countess looked at Jack and shrugged her shoulders, but didn't say anything.

'I haven't lost my marbles,' continued Madame Petrova, turning to the countess walking along beside her. 'Well, at least not all of them. Just a little eccentric perhaps. But that's allowed when you get to my age,' she added, chuckling. 'Ah, here's the first one.'

Jack pushed the wheelchair towards a bench under the oak tree and stopped.

'When we moved in here, many years ago now, we made a pact. There were six of us. All close friends. We had shared so much: the War, careers, lovers, tragedy.'

'What kind of pact?' asked Jack, sitting down on the bench next to the countess and facing Madame Petrova in the wheelchair.

'We agreed that whenever one of us – or one of our friends – passed away, we would plant an oak tree, right here. To remind us—'

'What a wonderful idea,' said Jack.

'I've planted twelve. This one here was the first one. It was planted in memory of my dear friend Marguerite, who set up this establishment. Sadly, she was the first one to leave us. This is her tree.'

Madame Petrova stopped and looked pensively up into the tree and the blue sky beyond. 'But the two trees that are perhaps most relevant as far as the little crosses are concerned,' she continued, speaking softly, 'are those two over there.'

Madame Petrova took a deep breath and pointed to a pair of trees standing a little apart from the others. 'The one on the left belongs to my sister, Anastasiya,' she said. 'She passed away just before the Coberg Mission closed. Let me to tell you about her.

'Our parents left Russia in 1915, before the Revolution, and came to live here in France. A far-sighted and fortuitous decision. We had a small chateau not far from here. My sister and I were both born there. Anastasiya was two years older. I became a ballet dancer and she became a concert pianist. An outstanding one. Then came the War and everything changed. I lived with my parents at the chateau at the time. Anastasiya stayed in Paris and fell in with the wrong crowd ...'

'What kind of wrong crowd?' prompted the countess.

'The Germans. They had everything. Power, glamour, wealth, rivers of champagne, fabulous uniforms. Everything. And they all lived in the Ritz in Paris, like Tsars. Reichsmarschall Göring had his headquarters there; holding court. It was the centre of power. And to some people, power is like an aphrodisiac, impossible to resist. Unfortunately, my sister was one of them. She was dazzled by the glamour – and that's when she met a dashing young SS officer at the Ritz. They fell in love, and she went to live with him there until the end of the war.'

Madame Petrova hesitated, and looked pensively at a swan gliding gracefully across the lake. 'And then I made a fateful decision ...'

'What kind of decision?' asked Jack.

'I went to live with my sister at the Ritz. It was the most exciting time of my life. But as we all know, nothing in life is free, and when you are a striking, twenty-two-year-old beauty, fawned over by powerful men twice your age, you don't know that.'

Madame Petrova put her hand on Jack's arm. 'The reason I'm telling you all this is because of the big price my sister had to pay. Just before the war ended, she became pregnant and had a girl, Natasha. As you can imagine, the Ritz wasn't a good place for a baby. And besides, the French considered the women cavorting with the Germans at the Ritz – the enemy – as traitors. Do you know what they called them?'

The countess shook her head.

'*Horizontals!* We all knew what was coming; the day of reckoning wasn't far away, and we also knew what the French Resistance did with traitors ... yet we partied like there was no tomorrow.'

'What happened?' asked Jack.

'The Third Reich was falling apart and the Germans were leaving Paris in a great hurry. My sister knew she couldn't stay behind. Because of her relationship with a high-ranking SS officer, she was well-known. Yet she couldn't go with him; not with a baby. That's when she made the most painful decision of her life ...'

'What decision?' asked the countess.

'She left her baby with me. The child and I were smuggled out of Paris by the SS, and taken to my parents at the chateau. Anastasiya left Paris with the Germans and we didn't hear from her for years. We didn't know if she was dead or alive. I went to live in London, and the child stayed with my parents and grew up at the chateau.'

'What happened to your sister?' asked the countess.

'A few years after the war ended, my parents received a letter from Australia. My sister had joined the Pallottines, and was living on a mission in Australia, teaching Aboriginal children. She was now known as Sister Elizabeth.'

'The Coberg Mission? asked Jack.

'Yes.'

Good God! thought Jack and paled, as the implications of what he had just heard began to sink in.

'And the SS officer; what happened to him?'

Madame Petrova shook her head. 'I don't know,' she said.

'And Natasha?' asked Jack, barely able to speak. 'What happened to her?'

'She was a delightful child – a bit of a tomboy. Always climbing trees and riding without a saddle; very cheeky. I visited her often. She was very artistic. After she left school, she became a photographer; a very gifted one.'

'Did she ever visit Australia, do you know?' asked Jack.

'She did. The article in the *National Geographic* you mentioned took her to Australia. It was her first big assignment. But that wasn't the only reason she went there ... She was looking for her parents.'

'What do you mean?' asked the countess.

'When Natasha turned twenty-one – that would have been in 1965; she was born in forty-four – my parents decided to tell her the truth about her parents, and what had happened to them. Until then, they had told her that her parents had been killed during the War. Two years later, she went to Australia, looking for her mother.'

'And found her at the Coberg Mission in Queensland?' interjected Jack.

Madame Petrova nodded.

'But that wasn't all, was it?' said Jack, sensing what was coming.

'No. Natasha stayed in Australia for a year. And while she was there, at the mission, she—'

'Had a child?'

Madame Petrova reached for Jack's hand and held it. 'Yes,' she whispered. 'And then history repeated itself ...'

'She gave up her child, and left it behind?' asked the countess, incredulous.

'Yes. With my sister's little cross around its little neck as the only ...' Overcome by emotion, Madame Petrova began to sob.

'But *why*?' asked the countess.

'We never found out.'

'What about the father?' said Jack.

Madame Petrova shook her head. 'Natasha didn't come back to France. She continued to travel the world. She was a free spirit and became an accomplished mountaineer and environmentalist – well ahead of her time. She climbed all the major peaks in the Himalayas and South America, and visited the Xingu Indians in the Amazon rainforest. Many of her photos and articles were published in magazines around the world. She had been inspired by Leni Riefenstahl—'

'Hitler's filmmaker?' interrupted the countess, taken aback.

'Yes.'

'What happened to Natasha?' whispered Jack.

Slowly, Madame Petrova lifted her hand and pointed to the second oak tree, her fingers shaking.

'When?'

'We don't know exactly. The last I heard, she was doing an assignment on the Nuba in the Sudan. The mysterious people of Kau. That was quite a few years ago. After that, she just disappeared ... I didn't hear from her again. I'm so sorry.'

'Do you know what happened?'

'Not really. There was a massacre in one of the villages ...'

Jack stood up, walked across to the oak tree and placed a hand on its trunk. Momentarily overwhelmed by sadness and grief, he placed his other hand on the little cross around his neck, and tried desperately not to cry.

Kuragin Chateau, Just Outside Paris: Christmas Eve 2012

Christmas Eve at the Kuragin Chateau had always been one of the highlights of the year. Outside, winter had arrived early. A heavy blanket of snow covered the grounds, turning the garden into a frozen wonderland of icicles and snowdrifts. The lake was frozen solid and the pine trees with their drooping branches looked like old men in fur coats, greeting the pale winter moon.

Inside, excitement and feverish activity filled the chateau and a mouth-watering aroma of roast goose and stewed apples drifted from the kitchen, promising a feast. Countess Kuragin walked into the music room and smiled. Jack stood on a ladder, dressing the Christmas tree. Her daughter, Anna, was handing him tinsel and coloured glass balls that had been in the family for more than a century, and Tristan was preparing the candles and coloured lights on the floor. Tristan, now a boy of fifteen, had come to live at the Kuragin Chateau after his mother was tragically killed during Anna's rescue two years earlier. The countess had taken the orphan into her heart and her home, and he had become a member of the family. He was going to school in a village nearby, and he and Jack had a special bond.

'How's it going?' said the countess.

'Only five hundred to go.'

'Can't be that bad. I can only see a dozen or so.'

'Look at the boxes over there.'

'Tree looks fabulous.'

'My arms are killing me, and so is my neck.'

'Why don't you take a break?'

'Are you kidding? I'm too stiff to climb down.'

'I have a surprise for you that will cheer you up; promise.'

'A few elves perhaps, to help me with this? That would cheer me up for sure.'

'Not elves; someone else…'

'What, *now?*' said Jack.

'No, in about an hour I'd say.'

'I may be dead by then.'

'Then you won't be eating the goose, I take it, nor the sweets?'

'On the other hand, I may try to stick around for a little longer.'

'I thought you might. Dinner at eight. You've got two hours.'

'You heard it, guys. We better get cracking!'

'Good plan,' said the countess and left the room.

Dr Alexandra Delacroix sat in the back seat of the chauffeur-driven hire car and watched the familiar landscape glide past. Charles de Gaulle airport on Christmas Eve had been chaotic and it had taken more than an hour just to get out of Paris. The heavy snow didn't help either.

Packing in a hurry and racing to Sydney airport was a blur, and so was the long flight. Accepting the countess's invitation to join the family in France for Christmas had been a spur of the moment decision. Exhausted by weeks of relentless work at the Gordon Institute in Sydney, Alexandra had slept through most of the flight. It had been her first opportunity to relax a little after the groundbreaking discovery of Demexilyn, a new immunotherapy drug that was a Professor K-inspired game-changer.

François, the countess's butler-cum-chauffeur, saw the car cross the moat and approach the front gate. 'She's here,' he said to the countess.

'Just in time; we are about to sit down to dinner. Take her through the back door and then bring her straight to the dining room. It will be a nice surprise.'

'Done.'

'This is for Father Christmas, I take it?' said Jack, pointing to the empty seat beside him.

'Wrong gender. Patience; remember I promised you a surprise?' said the countess.

'A surprise guest?'

'Hm ...'

'How intriguing.'

Jack sat back in his chair and soaked up the festive atmosphere in the large, elegant dining room. The marble fireplace and the mirror above had been decorated with garlands of tinsel and angel hair, reflecting the candlelight. Rustic baskets on the mantelpiece full of shiny red apples and walnuts painted gold and silver, conjured up memories of hot Christmas Days spent on the family farm in Queensland in forty degree heat, celebrated on the veranda with loved ones, now long gone.

Then someone dimmed the lights, the door opened and Alexandra burst into the room, her face flushed with excitement. Jolted from his memories, Jack just stared at her for a moment, not quite trusting his eyes as the room erupted in spontaneous applause. Then his face lit up as he walked over to Alexandra and embraced her.

'I thought I'd do a Jack Rogan and surprise everyone. Merry Christmas,' said Alexandra and kissed Jack on the cheek.

'Wow! This *is* a Christmas present. I had no idea – wonderful to see you.'

The countess looked at Jack and winked.

Jack took Alexandra by the hand. 'Come, let me introduce you to someone special.' He pointed to a petite, beautifully dressed old lady sitting in the chair next to his. 'This is Madame Petrova, my great-aunt.'

'Enchanted,' said Madame Petrova, extending a bony hand with a stunning diamond ring fit for a Tsarina on her ring finger. 'I've heard a lot about you. Come, sit next to me.'

After the excitement had died down a little, the countess stood up and raised her glass. 'To absent friends,' she said. 'Merry Christmas!'

'Merry Christmas,' echoed the others. Moments later, dinner was served and the exquisite wines especially chosen by the countess began to flow, ensuring the Christmas cheer stayed cheerful and never lost momentum.

After dinner, the guests retired to the music room to watch the lighting of the Christmas tree and open presents. Alexandra knew all who were there, but she missed her parents, who were attending a medical conference in New York. Anna was sitting at the piano playing Christmas carols, and others were singing along.

Alexandra turned to the countess. 'Where's Jack?' she asked, looking around the crowded room full of excited faces.

'Come quickly, I'll show you.'

The countess took Alexandra by the hand and they hurried to the entrance foyer together. 'There,' she said, pointing to the large open staircase leading to the upper floors.

Jack stood on a landing, carrying Madame Petrova in his arms.

She had one arm around his neck and was looking adoringly up at him. As there was no lift in the chateau and she couldn't walk up the stairs to the bedrooms, Jack had decided to carry her up instead.

'It's been a long time since a young man swept me off my feet,' said Madame Petrova. 'This is my Christmas present; perhaps my last one.'

'No way!' said Jack. 'Now that I've found you, we'll celebrate many more together, just you watch.'

'In that case, please make sure you don't drop me.'

'Don't worry, you're as light as a feather.'

Alexandra looked at the countess, tears in her eyes. 'I'm so happy for him; let's leave them to it. We'll never forget this,' she whispered and tiptoed back into the shadows.

Alexandra opened the door to the little chapel at the back of the chateau and looked inside. Jack was sitting in a pew at the front. It was well past midnight. A few candles spluttering next to a small Christmas tree on the altar sent crazy shadows dancing along the stone floor and up the walls, like angels celebrating.

'I thought I'd find you here,' said Alexandra and sat down next to Jack. 'Do you mind?'

'Of course not. It's been quite a night.'

'Sure has.'

'Christmas is like that. It stirs up the past.'

'And emotions and memories we like to keep locked up during the year,' added Alexandra.

'Quite so.'

Jack reached inside his shirt and pulled out the little cross. 'Strange how this little cross has finally led me to my mother,' said Jack, the sadness in his voice obvious, 'and to a great-aunt I didn't know I had, until too late.'

Alexandra reached for Jack's hand and squeezed it. 'Certain things are meant to be.'

'Perhaps Gurrul was right. Certain things are best left alone.'

'You couldn't do that, Jack; not you. You of all people had to know.'

'Well, at least now I know who my mother was, and that's great. But everything I know about my father is purely circumstantial. Still too many questions.'

'Perhaps not so …'

Jack looked at Alexandra. 'What do you mean?' he asked.

'It's freezing in here; let's go somewhere else.'

Jack took Alexandra to the large kitchen in the basement, which only a short time ago had been a hive of Christmas activity. A mouth-watering aroma of roast goose and spices still hung in the air, and a teacake had been left on the refectory table in front of the huge stone fireplace for late-night visitors looking for a snack.

Jack pointed to the table, polished smooth and shiny around the edges by countless elbows. 'This is my favourite spot; the cosiest place in the entire chateau, and the most popular.' he said. 'Cook never lets the fire go out and always leaves a tasty morsel next to the urn here. Isn't it beautiful?'

'What is it?'

'It's a samovar, for making tea. It's been in the Kuragin family forever. A tea urn warming generations, she calls it. This is where she first told me about Anna and her disappearance. This is where it all began. Tea?'

'Yes please,' said Alexandra. 'And it's difficult to believe that it was only a year ago we met right here at the chateau just after Professor K died, and I was travelling to Sydney to take up my appointment at the Gordon.'

'And I suggested we travel to Sydney together—'

'And you invited me to stay in your apartment, just like that.'

'And you moved in, just like that. With a dangerous bloke ...'

'Well, I didn't know that at the time, did I?'

'So much has happened in a year. Your adventure with Blackburn Pharmaceuticals, your abduction ...' said Jack.

'Alistair Macbeth and your brush with death in Somalia.'

'At least it wasn't in vain.'

'No, it wasn't. You brought down the British government.'

'And you discovered a groundbreaking new drug.'

Alexandra nodded. 'Professor K's legacy.'

For a while, Jack and Alexandra sat in silence, sipping tea and watching the embers glow in the fireplace like the eyes of demons, watching.

'I have a Christmas present for you,' said Alexandra. 'A bittersweet one ...'

'Oh?' Jack looked at Alexandra, intrigued. 'What is it?'

'Certainty.'

'How interesting. Care to elaborate?'

A few months after taking up her appointment at the Gordon, Alexandra had told Jack about the amazing progress in DNA sequencing and the impact the new, revolutionary technology had had on forensics. It was in that context that Jack had mentioned the bloodstains on the mural in Bryn Evans's prison cell.

'Remember our discussion about the bloodstains?' said Alexandra.

'Sure do. You said it was possible, but a long shot. If you could extract DNA from the traces of remaining blood, we could perhaps—'

'Find out if—'

'If Bryn was my father.'

'Correct. And then you went back to the prison in Fremantle.'

'I did.'

'To get that sample we talked about.'

Jack smiled as he remembered what happened. When the tour reached Bryn's cell, he made sure he was the last one to go inside. Then, pretending to be taking a close-up, he knelt down and, holding his camera close to the mural, quickly scraped off a small sample of the bloodstained plaster with a penknife and placed it in a small plastic bag. That was several weeks ago. As he hadn't heard back from Alexandra, Jack had assumed the exercise was unsuccessful.

Jack looked at Alexandra. 'I thought this was supposed to be some kind of Christmas present, not torture.'

'All right, here it is: The DNA test was successful.'

'And—?'

'I can categorically state that the man whose blood we examined, was your biological father.'

Jack looked thunderstruck. 'My God! *Are you sure?*'

'Absolutely!'

Jack leaned across the table and embraced Alexandra. 'Thank you,' he whispered. 'I can't tell you how much this means to me.'

'I know.'

'All the pieces are falling into place. This confirms everything. This is *proof.*'

'Looks that way.'

'An exquisite Fabergé cross and a priceless pearl; a handsome Welsh pearler; and an adventurous young Russian aristocrat with a reckless streak.'

'And don't forget Sister Elizabeth, your grandmother,' said Alexandra.

Jack shook his head. 'And to think that I grew up only an hour's ride from the mission without knowing ...'

'Couldn't have been easy for her. Staying away, I mean. She must have loved you very much.'

'You're right.'

'What about Brother Francis?'

'Was he the dashing SS officer from the Ritz in Paris she fell in love with, you mean? *Was he my grandfather?*'

Alexandra nodded.

'You have no idea how often I've asked myself this question. All the pieces seem to fit. But we'll never know for sure, will we?'

'I suppose not. But does it really matter?'

'Not really.'

'What an exciting family you didn't know you had – until now,' said Alexandra, a mischievous sparkle in her eyes. 'It explains a lot.'

'What do you mean, "it explains a lot"; about what?'

'*You!* Why you are such an—'

'What?'

'Incorrigible rascal!'

'That's a little harsh.'

'Is it?'

'Okay. But *lovable*, right?'

Alexandra took her time before answering, letting Jack sweat. Then she leaned over to him and put an arm around his neck. '*Sometimes.* Merry Christmas Jack,' she whispered, and kissed him tenderly on the forehead.

THREE MONTHS LATER: COBERG MISSION; MARCH 2013

Jack jumped off his horse, took off his hat and looked around. The Coberg Mission had been closed down many years ago, and a recent bushfire had done considerable damage to the deserted buildings. Most of the roofs had caved in, some of the walls and chimneys had collapsed, and the dirt road had been completely washed away during a summer storm a long time ago. However, the little chapel, which stood apart from the other buildings, looked just as he remembered.

Jack took a small metal container out of his saddlebag and slowly walked up the hill to the little cemetery behind the chapel. *They are all here,* he thought as he looked at the small gravestones set out in neat rows close to each other. All the Pallottine brothers and sisters who died at the mission over the years were buried there. The headstones had no surnames and no dates of birth, only a small cross at the top, the first name of the brother or sister, and the date of death. Jack walked along the rows, looking for two specific graves.

Brother Francis was buried next to Sister Elizabeth in the last row. *I suppose that says it all,* thought Jack and reached for the little cross he wore around his neck and never took off. For a while he stood in silence as he remembered his father's death eleven years ago that had started it all. Then he turned away from the graves and looked pensively across to the barren ridge shimmering in the distance, and the familiar plains he had explored on horseback as a boy with Gurrul.

As he looked at the little box in his hand, Jack's mind drifted back to the strange telephone call from Gurrul's nephew in Wyndham two weeks earlier:

'Gurrul's dead, mate. He died suddenly yesterday in the bush, just like that. I was there.'

'What happened?'

'He had some kind of fit and then ... Just before he died, he asked if you would take him home,' said the nephew.

'What do you mean, *home?*'

'To the Coberg Mission. Can you do it?'

'Sure.'

Jack opened the little metal box containing Gurrul's ashes and slowly emptied the contents on top of a rock next to Brother Francis's headstone. Then he stood back and smiled as he remembered his friend's face: furrowed like the parched outback earth and with deep creases and wrinkles crisscrossing his forehead that looked as if they could hold three days' rain.

Jack watched as the morning breeze suddenly picked up and began to blow Gurrul's ashes down the hill and across the plain, returning them to where they belonged.

***

More Books by the Author

The Empress Holds the Key (Jack Rogan Mysteries Book 1)
The Disappearance of Anna Popov (Jack Rogan Mysteries Book 2)
The Hidden Genes of Professor K (Jack Rogan Mysteries Book 3)
Professor K: The Final Quest (Jack Rogan Mysteries Book 4)
The Curious Case of the Missing Head (Jack Rogan Mysteries Book 5)
The Lost Symphony (Jack Rogan Mysteries Book 6)
The Death Mask Murders (Jack Rogan Mysteries Book 7)
The Stolen Altarpiece (Jack Rogan Mysteries Book 8)

THE EMPRESS HOLD THE KEY

A disturbing, edge-of-your-seat historical
mystery thriller

Jack Rogan Mysteries Book 1

**Dark secrets. A holy relic. An ancient quest
reignited.**

Jack Rogan's discovery of a disturbing old photograph in the ashes of
a rural Australian cottage draws the journalist into a dangerous hunt
with the ultimate stakes.

The tangled web of clues – including hoards of Nazi gold, hidden
Swiss bank accounts, and a long-forgotten mass grave – implicate
wealthy banker Sir Eric Newman and lead to a trial with shocking
revelations.

A holy relic mysteriously erased from the pages of history is
suddenly up for grabs to those willing to sacrifice everything to find it.
Rogan and his companions must follow historical leads through
ancient Egypt, to the Crusades and the Knights Templar, to uncover a
secret that could destroy the foundations of the Catholic Church and
challenge the history of Christianity itself.

Will Rogan succeed in bringing the dark mystery into the light, or
will the powers desperately working against him ensure the ancient
truths remain buried forever?

The Empress Holds the Key
is now available in ebook and paperback

THE DISAPPEARANCE OF ANNA POPOV

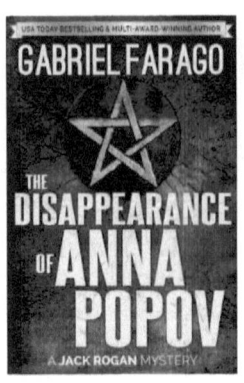

A dark, page-turning psychological thriller

Jack Rogan Mysteries Book 2

A mysterious disappearance. An outlaw bikie gang. One dangerous investigation.

Journalist Jack Rogan cannot resist a good mystery. When he stumbles across a hidden clue about the tragic disappearance of two girls from Alice Springs years earlier, he's determined to investigate.

Joining forces with his New York literary agent; a retired Aboriginal police officer; and Cassandra, an enigmatic psychic, Rogan enters the dark and dangerous world of an outlaw bikie gang ruled by an evil master.

Entangled in a web of violence, superstition and fear, Rogan and his friends follow the trail of the missing girls into the remote Dreamtime-wilderness of outback Australia, where they face their greatest challenge yet.

Cassandra has a secret agenda of her own and uses her occult powers to conjure up an epic showdown where the stakes are high, and the loser faces death and oblivion.

Will Rogan succeed in finding the truth, or will the forces of evil prevail, causing untold misery and destroying even more lives?

Gold Medal Winner in Psychological Mysteries
- Thriller Category
The Global Book Awards 2022

The Disappearance of Anna Popov
is now available in ebook and paperback

THE HIDDEN GENES OF PROFESSOR K

A dark, disturbing and nail-biting medical thriller

Jack Rogan Mysteries Book 3

A medical breakthrough. A greedy pharmaceutical magnate. A brutal double-murder. One tangled web of lies.

World-renowned scientist Professor K is close to a groundbreaking discovery. He's also dying. With his last breath, he anoints Dr Alexandra Delacroix as his successor and pleads with her to carry on his work.

But powerful forces will stop at nothing to possess the research, unwittingly plunging Delacroix into a treacherous world of unbridled ambition and greed.

Desperate and alone, she turns to celebrated author and journalist Jack Rogan.

Rogan must help Delacroix, while also assisting famous rock star Isis in the seemingly unrelated investigation into the brutal murder of her parents.

With the support of Isis's resourceful PA, Lola; a former police officer; a tireless campaigner for the destitute and forgotten; and a gifted boy with psychic powers, Rogan exposes a complex web of fiercely guarded secrets and heinous crimes of the past that can ruin them all and change history.

Will the dreams of a visionary scientist with the power to change the future of medicine fall into the wrong hands, or will his genius benefit mankind and prevent untold misery and suffering for generations to come?

"Outstanding Thriller" of 2017
Independent Author Network Book of the Year Awards

The Hidden Genes of Professor K
is now available in ebook and paperback

PROFESSOR K:
THE FINAL QUEST

An action-packed historical medical mystery

Jack Rogan Mysteries Book 4

A desperate plea from the Vatican. A kidnapped chef. An ambitious mob boss. One perilous game.

When Professor Alexandra Delacroix is called in to find a cure for the dying pope, she follows clues left by her mentor and friend, the late Professor K, which lead her on a breathtaking search through historical secrets, some of them deadly.

Her old friend Jack Rogan must step in to assist while also searching for kidnapped Top Chef Europe winner Lorenza da Baggio.

He joins forces with his young friend and gifted psychic, Tristan; a dedicated Mafia-hunting prosecutor; a fearless young police officer; and an enigmatic Egyptian detective who is on a perilous hunt for a notorious IS terrorist.

Together, they stand off with the head of a powerful Mafia family in Florence and uncover a network of corruption and heinous crimes reaching to the very top.

Will Rogan and his friends succeed in finding Lorenza and curing the pope, or will the dark forces swirling around them prevail in their sinister plots?

Gold Medal Winner in the Fiction – Thriller – Medical Category
Readers' Favorite 2019 International Book Awards Contest

Professor K: The Final Quest
is now available ebook and paperback

The Curious Case
of the Missing Head

A gripping medical thriller

Jack Rogan Mysteries Book 5

A headless body on a boat. An international conspiracy. Can a kidnapped genius survive a controversial scientific discovery?
Esteemed Australian journalist Jack Rogan is on a mission to solve the disappearance of his mother in the 70s. But when a friend needs help rescuing a kidnapped world-renowned astrophysicist, he doesn't hesitate. Struggling with more questions than answers, his investigation leads them aboard a hellish hospital ship, where instead of finding the kidnap victim, he's confronted with a decapitated corpse.

As the search intensifies, Jack bumps up against diabolical cartels with hidden agendas. And when his research reveals dubious experiments, a criminal on death row, and a shocking revelation about his mother's fate, he must uncover how it's all linked.

Can Jack unravel the twisted connections and catch the scientist's killer, or will the next obituary published be his own?

Gold Medal Winner in the Fiction – Thriller – Conspiracy Category
Readers' Favorite 2020 International Book Awards Contest

"Outstanding Thriller/Suspense" - Category Winner of 2020
Independent Author Network Book of the Year Awards

The Curious Case of the Missing Head
is now available ebook and paperback

THE LOST SYMPHONY

A historical mystery thriller

Jack Rogan Mysteries Book 6

A murdered tsarina. A lost musical master-piece. A stolen Russian icon. Can Jack honour a promise made a long time ago, and solve an age-old mystery?

When acclaimed Australian journalist and author Jack Rogan inherits an old music box with a curious letter hidden inside, he decides to investigate. As he delves deeper into a murky past of secrets and violence, he soon discovers he's not the only one interested in solving the puzzle.

Frieda Malenkova, a ruthless art dealer; and Victor Sokolov, a Russian billionaire with a dark past, will stop at nothing to achieve their dark desires and foil Jack's valiant struggle to uncover the truth.

Joining forces with Mademoiselle Darrieux, a flamboyant Paris socialite; and Claude Dupree, a retired French police officer, Jack enters a dangerous world of unbridled ambition, murder and greed that threatens to destroy him.

On a perilous journey that takes him deep into Russia, Jack follows a tortuous path of discovery, disappointment and betrayal that brings him face to face with his destiny.

Will Jack unravel the hidden clues left behind by a desperate empress? Can he save the precious legacy of a genius before it's too late, and return a holy icon revered by generations to where it belongs?

Gold Medal Winner in the Fiction – Mystery – Historical Category
Readers' Favorite 2021 International Book Awards Contest

Award-Winning Finalist in the Fiction: Thriller/Adventure Category
The 2021 International Book Awards

"Outstanding Mystery" of 2021 - Category Winner
Independent Author Network Book of the Year Awards

The Lost Symphony
is now available in ebook and paperback

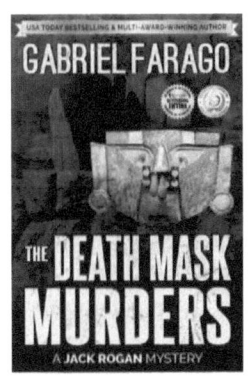

THE DEATH MASK MURDERS

A historical mystery crime thriller

Jack Rogan Mysteries Book 7

Seven brutal murders. A cursed Inca burial mask. A lost treasure. One deadly game.

When convicted killer Maurice Landru reaches out from a Paris prison and asks for help to prove his innocence, celebrated author Jack Rogan cannot resist. Drawn into a web of hidden clues pointing to an ancient mystery, Jack decides to investigate.

Joining forces with Francesca Bartolli, a glamorous criminal profiler; Mademoiselle Darrieux, an eccentric Paris socialite; and Claude Dupree, a retired French police officer, Jack enters a dangerous world of depraved cyber-gambling, where the stakes are high and the players will stop at nothing to satisfy their dark desires.

Following his 'breadcrumbs of destiny', Jack soon comes up against an evil genius who terminates his enemies without mercy and is prepared to risk all to win.

On a perilous journey littered with violence and death, Jack uncovers dark secrets of a murky past of ruthless conquistadors, bloodthirsty pirates and shipwrecked priests, all pointing to a fabulous treasure, waiting to be discovered.

Can Jack expose the mastermind behind the horrific murders and retrieve the legendary treasure before it falls into the wrong hands, or will the forces of darkness overwhelm him and destroy everything he believes in?

Gold Medal Winner in the Fiction - Mystery - Historical Category
Readers' Favorite 2022 International Book Awards Contest

"Outstanding Mystery" of 2022 - Mystery Category Winner
Independent Author Network Book of the Year Awards

The Death Mask Murders
is now available in ebook and paperback

THE STOLEN ALTARPIECE

A historical mystery crime thriller
Jack Rogan Mysteries Book 8

A long-forgotten amulet. A stolen painting. A dark threat reignited. One deadly geopolitical power-play.

Jack Rogan's discovery of a hidden letter reaching out of the past unwittingly embarks the journalist into a perilous quest to find a holy relic that has the power to fight evil.

As he follows a web of intriguing clues that take him on a dangerous journey to the Middle East, Rogan soon crosses swords with an old adversary, who is determined to destroy him and those he holds dear.

Soon, secrets buried in a famous stolen painting point to Russia and the threat of war in Ukraine. Joining forces with Tristan, a gifted psychic; Abbot Serapion, a Russian monk; and Sasha, the daughter of a Russian billionaire, Jack enters a dangerous geopolitical arena ruled by a deranged, corrupt man consumed by unbridled ambition and lust for power, who threatens to enslave a nation and destroy an entire country to satisfy his misguided vision of greatness.

Can Jack find a way to defeat the dark forces of evil and turn the tide of history before it's too late, or will the horrors of war continue, and consume a people who dared to stand against tyranny and dream of freedom?

Gold Medal Winner in the Fiction - Thriller - Political Category
Readers' Favorite 2023 International Book Awards Contest

Gold Medal Winner in Amateur Sleuth - Thriller Category
The Global Book Awards 2023

"Outstanding Mystery" of 2023 Category Winner
Independent Author Network Book of the Year Awards

ABOUT THE AUTHOR

Gabriel Farago is the *USA TODAY* bestselling and multi-award-winning Australian author of *The Jack Rogan Mysteries Series* for the thinking reader.

As a lawyer with a passion for history and archaeology, Gabriel Farago had to wait many years before being able to pursue another passion – writing – in earnest. However, his love of books and story-telling started long before that.

'I remember as a young boy reading biographies and history books with a torch under the bed covers,' he recalls, 'and then writing stories about archaeologists and explorers the next day, instead of doing homework. While I regularly got into trouble for this, I believe we can only do well in our endeavours if we are passionate about the things we love. For me, writing has become a passion.'

Born in Budapest, Gabriel grew up in postwar Europe and, after fleeing Hungary with his parents during the Revolution in 1956, he went to school in Austria before arriving in Australia as a teenager. This allowed him to become multilingual and feel 'at home' in different countries and diverse cultures.

Shaped by a long legal career and experiences spanning several decades and continents, his is a mature voice that speaks in many tongues. Gabriel holds degrees in literature and law, speaks several languages and takes research and authenticity very seriously. Inquisitive by nature, he studied Egyptology and learned to read the hieroglyphs. He travels extensively and visits all the locations mentioned in his books.

'I try to weave fact and fiction into a seamless storyline,' he explains. 'By blurring the boundaries between the two, the reader is never quite sure where one ends, and the other begins. This is, of course, quite deliberate, as it creates the illusion of authenticity and reality in a work that is pure fiction. A successful work of fiction is a balancing act: reality must rub shoulders with imagination in a way that is both entertaining and plausible.'

Gabriel lives just outside Sydney, Australia, in the Blue Mountains, surrounded by a World Heritage National Park. 'The beauty and solitude of this unique environment,' he points out, 'gives me the inspiration and energy to weave my thoughts and ideas into stories that in turn, I sincerely hope, will entertain and inspire my readers.'

Gabriel Farago

Author's Note

I hope you enjoyed reading this book as much as I enjoyed writing it. I'd be very grateful if you'd post a short review on Amazon. Your support really does make a difference.

Connect with the Author

Amazon
https://www.amazon.com/stores/
Gabriel-Farago/author/B00GUVY2UW

Website
https://gabrielfarago.com.au/

Goodreads
https://www.goodreads.com/author/show/7435911.Gabriel_Farago

Facebook
https://www.facebook.com/GabrielFaragoAuthor

BookBub
https://www.bookbub.com/profile/gabriel-farago